In Turmoil

Stories

Sushil Chadha

Publishers
UNICORN BOOKS
F-2/16, Ansari Road, Daryaganj, New Delhi-110002
☎ Ph.: 011-23275434, 23262683, 23250704
E-mail: info@unicornbooks.in • *Website:* www.unicornbooks.in

Branch : Mumbai
23-25, Zaoba Wadi, Thakurdwar, Mumbai-400002
☎ 022-22010941, 022-22053387
E-mail: unicornbooksmumbai@gmail.com

ISBN 978-81-7806-569-4

Edition: 2020

Printed at : Param Offsetters, Okhla, New Delhi-110020

When I meet God, I am going to ask him two questions: Why relativity and why turbulence? I really believe he will have an answer for the first.

Werner Heisenberg

For my grandsons,
Arav and Advay

In Turmoil

Contents

Plunder

The moment I learnt about the auction of the Kwatras' personal belongings, I was in a tizzy. I could not concentrate in the class and repeatedly looked at my watch. Some of the sweetest memories of my childhood are entwined with the Kwatras. Whatever I am today, I owe it to them. I rushed from the class, kicked the motorbike and crossed the main gate of the school even before the last bell rang. I drove straight to Vasant Kunj, Sector A.

My association with the Kwatras dates back to 1985, when I was struggling with arithmetic in class five. My mother ironed the clothes on a table installed near the stairs of the Kwatras block and it was my responsibility, being the eldest of two brothers and two sisters, to collect the clothes from various houses and return them in the evening after mother had ironed them.

I saw little of my father for he worked as a road construction labourer in different parts of northern India. He had planned my career in cement and mortar in the hope that I would join at a slightly better position. We lived about two kilometres away, in the inner winding lane of Mehrauli, where wafts of fresh air never strayed in and sunlight never shone. We preferred the open sky near our mother's table, created spaces around it, played and skipped on the stairs; it was a surrogate home for us. All of us left Mehrauli in the morning and returned in the evening; during the day I attended the corporation school nearby.

Mr. Kwatra had retired recently as under secretary, Ministry of Education. He had a passion for mathematics and wanted to be a lecturer but circumstances forced him to join as a clerk. After retirement, he wanted to do what he had missed out in life — to teach mathematics. He collected servants' children and bribed them with chocolates to attend the classes in the afternoon for an hour or two. My mother implored him to take me under his wing, to which Mr. Kwatra readily agreed and was equally grateful as the number of the children had dwindled from six to three and he was in danger of closing down his school.

Mrs. Kwatra was responsible for the diminishing numbers. Easily irascible, she had a sharp tongue and did not hesitate to fling the choicest of Punjabi abuses at the children if other tactics failed. A vice-principal in a government school, she faced the ill clad, filthy school children for seven-eight hours a day and her blood boiled on seeing them at home as well.

Short, fair, bald, with a round belly, a pleasant kindly face given to uninhibited laughter, and bright eyes, Mr. Kwatra hopped like a frog in front of the black board (one of the bedrooms was converted into a classroom), his face suffused with intelligence and happiness. At the end of the class, his clothes were smeared with chalk; there was more of it on the shirt and the floor than on the board. With a polite smile, he would dust off the layers of chalk and then one of us, mostly I was the privileged one, would clean up the room lest Mr. Kwatra got a taste of his wife's lashing tongue. He played around with numbers and infused life in them; gave a pat on my back or an imperceptible frown if I did not react properly to his instructions. All the students looked forward to his afternoon classes more than the school. Within a few months, arithmetic became my favourite subject.

Mrs. Kwatra was slim, slightly taller and a shade darker than her husband. She had a grave countenance, piercing eyes and full lips, which did not break into a smile easily. But she carried herself with dignity. For the first few months, I was so afraid of her that I religiously avoided running into her. Often, she reprimanded her husband. "You are wasting your time. Nothing can change their lives — they will all end up as servants."

One day when she was at it again, I plucked some courage, looked up and said, "Auntieji, I want to be a teacher — like you." There was something in my manner — a little rebellion, a little pride — that she stopped ranting, sat down on her favourite chair and looked straight into my eyes. There was a sparkle in the eyes that used to scare me earlier. She ruffled my uncouth hair and whispered softly, "You will be!" And then her face creased into a smile.

That incident brought a metamorphic change in her and we established a special bond. After school, I found myself more at the Kwatras home rather than helping out my mother with clothes. Mrs. Kwatra told me stories from the Mahabharata, Ramayana, and Panchtantra and I sat glued to the carpet and listened to every word of hers with rapt attention. Sometimes, as a bonus, I was allowed to watch a movie on the newly purchased colour TV.

She talked of her son and daughter (both settled abroad), her school principal, colleagues, relatives and friends with more ease with me than with her husband. With a sweet smile, a wide -eyed look and unmatched patience, I was able to bridge the gap of half a century. Sensitive by nature, I was able to appreciate her varying moods and was responsive to her reflexes. Her fiery outburst told me that she had lost out on promotion.

Three months later she told her husband, "Look Satish, my own children have forgotten my birthday this time. But Sudhir has remembered and presented me this beautiful card." I refused to tell her where I had got the money from as I had stolen it from my mother's drawer. The Kwatras showered their affection, gave me clothes, presents and virtually adopted me. Mrs. Kwatra had the foresight and vision; she fired me with ambition. "One day you will be a professor like my son," she assured me. My grades improved; I got over 70% marks in senior secondary and was able to get admission in Deshbandu College in Maths (Honours).

During the summer vacation, the whole family went to Punjab for two months to attend the marriage of my cousin. On return, I learnt that Mrs. Kwatra had died of a heart attack and their son had taken Mr. Kwatra to the States. My world came tumbling down. I would look up at the balcony many a time, hoping to see Mrs. Kwatra's smiling face. The dreams she had spun for me materialized only partially. Though I got a position in the university in Honours, I was not able to do equally well in post graduation and was forced to become a teacher in Springdales School. Last year, I married my colleague Gita, who is insistent I should join M. Phil and become a lecturer.

When I reached the Kwatras house, I found unusual activity. About thirty people, mostly women, were moving around in the house. A score of maids, chowkidars, and gardeners from whom I had distanced over the years, thanks to Kwatras, were at the bottom of the stairs. They were staring at the house with excitement, in the hope that they will be lucky to grab something.

From the gossip I learnt that the daughter-in-law had sold the house and was disposing off the belongings. I clambered up the stairs, entered the house (after more than ten years) and was sorry to see the pathetic plight of the house. During the Kwatras' times, it had a cheerful look — fresh flowers in the rooms, bottle palms in the corners and the walls embellished with bright oil canvasses.

The saleable items were neatly arranged with labels indicating the minimum price. In many cases, the prices had been slashed repeatedly to ensure their disposal. A large number of articles bore signs of 'sold'. The carpet on which I had squatted so often and listened to the stories had been sold for Rs 500. The dull brownish grey sofa set was sold for a thousand rupees.

Memories from the past flooded me as I walked around the house, looking at the various things on display. I had grown up amongst those very objects; some of them had been bought either in my presence or after my coming into contact with the Kwatras. I vividly remembered a bleak, cloudy day in December; Mrs. Kwatra was very low, surrounded by gloomy thoughts when I suggested that I wanted to eat pakoras.

In a trice, she was transformed. She was all vitality, telephoning the bakery, ordering me around to do this and that. She was very possessive of a corning dinner set gifted by her son and refused to take it out even on the rare parties they threw. She made an exception this time and the three of us had a merry feast of pastries, patties and pakoras. But the corning set was not for sale. None of the ladies, looking up and down at the items, could associate warm, rich emotions with them. My sweet remembrances were trampled as they haggled with a young man about the price. But he stolidly refused and pointed towards a tall lady talking with a prospective client, her back facing me.

Mrs. Kwatra had a weakness for silks and she looked very elegant whenever she dressed for a party. Most of the Kanjiwarm silk saris displayed were priced at Rs. 500 to Rs.1000. There was one in a flaming orange colour that I liked and had complimented her when she wore it. It was pegged at 400 and I had less than a hundred in my wallet. Suddenly, I had a keen desire to buy it for Gita, though I was not sure whether she would approve of it. I made my way through the crowd towards the daughter-in-law.

Dressed in faded jeans and a red striped top, she appeared to be in her early thirties. She talked to her customers with ease but did not appear to be a part of the crowd. A first generation Indian settled in the States, she had the impudence of an American. She smiled professionally, the smile widened when she accepted the money on finalisation of the deal. Apprehensively, I approached her, introduced myself and asked about Mr. Kwatra. "He is OK," she replied casually looking at the other clients. Her tone was not encouraging. I hung around for some time, then took the plunge and told her about my predicament and promised to give the money by late evening. Her gaze went up and down trying to assess me and I felt embarrassed. "Oh, you are Sudhir, the servant boy with a flair for maths," she said and smiled.

I used to perform many menial chores but the Kwatras never made me feel I was a servant in their house. Stunned, my knees felt weak. It was as if my roots had suddenly snapped. "I am sorry but you have to bring ready cash." She smiled again and turned to another customer.

I sank down on a chair bearing a 'sold` label. I imagined the room full of smells and noises from the past — the clatter of chappal and sandal as the Kwatras walked around, Mr. Kwatra's loud laughter, Mrs. Kwatra's shouting, "Sudhir, Sudhir", the noise of food being prepared and the smell of omelette, halwa and vegetables emanating from the kitchen. However, they were drowned in the continuous chattering and sniping of women.

I was keen to buy a little souvenir in the memory of the Kwatras and though the prices were being reduced every half an hour, nothing was likely to fall within my range. Frustrated, I left the house, went down the stairs and leaned against the tree just opposite the stairs, reflecting on my stupidity for carrying such a small amount in my wallet.

An hour later, the daughter-in-law, accompanied by two servants, brought two big cardboard boxes full of the Kwatras belongings, which had not been priced and threw them on the street. "This is free," she raised her voice addressing the servants. She smiled at me meaningfully as she ascended the stairs.

The interminable wait had flagged the servant's interest. But on seeing the boxes, they excitedly pounced on the two heaps. There were old pair of shoes, sandals, torn books, a box of chalk, terracotta and plaster of Paris idols of Ganesha, Laxmi, Buddha, a few dolls, leather horses from Rajasthan, a few watches, dozens of ball pens, hangers, and a large number of broken wooden, and steel photo frames. In the scuffle, someone grabbed a piece of shoe, the other a sandal, a leg of Ganesha, the other its head. It was a poignant sight. Human bodies pushing, jostling and wrestling with one another. Everyone had a bit of the Kwatras in their hands for use or display. I felt devastated.

The daughter-in-law appeared again. Her refulgent face was now showing signs of disintegration. With a broken glass frame in her hand, she descended a few steps and looked at the street to find some space where she could throw it. In the process, she cut her thumb and a few drops of blood dropped onto the stairs. "Shit," she said hoarsely and hurled the frame in the middle of the street. It fell with a thud, a few yards away from me. The glass splinters splashed across the street, a few struck my shoes.

For a moment, a hush swept across the street. The women and children stopped picking up the leftovers, and looked coldly at her.

Disturbed by the noise, the street dog sleeping under the shade of the Peepal tree at a little distance, opened its eyes, and shook its head and ears.

There was something vaguely familiar about the size and colour of the frame. I walked over and picked it up. I had clicked the Kwatras when I was in the first year of college and presented the framed photograph to them on their marriage anniversary. How could she treat the photograph of the old couple in this shabby manner?

Smouldering under the insult, I glared hard at her, my eyes flashing fire. The dog walked casually over the glass splinters, moved towards the stairs and suddenly barked at the woman responsible for orchestrating the show. She withdrew and went up the stairs.

I removed the glass pieces sticking to the photograph, cleaned it with my hanky, slipped the memories of Kwatras in the deep abyss of my heart and walked towards the motorbike.

■■■

Ties

"Sir, there is some Mrs. S. Dubey on the line. She says she knows you since college days."

Slouched on the sofa after lunch, Shekhar Aggarwal, Deputy Collector, Customs, Indira Gandhi International Airport, Delhi, drawled nonchalantly. "I don't remember her, but put her on line."

There was a click of switches. "Shekhar, I am Shivani. How are you?"

"Oh, Shivani!"

Dazed, he sat upright on the sofa.

"I want to meet you today; Standard at 6p.m. Will that do?" Her voice was crisp, business like.

"Yes, but Shivani—."

The line was dead. He looked vaguely at the receiver and reluctantly put it back. The voice from the past — which he had heard after nearly twenty five years — jolted him. Varied emotions hit him simultaneously.

He told the P.A to cancel the appointments, and switched on the red light. Memories of Shivani flipped backward and forward, the images were juxtaposed, the pain they brought was real. It tore him apart. A cup of black coffee alleviated his suffering and cleared the haze.

Returning home in the bus, one afternoon, he noticed a strikingly pretty girl dressed in a long skirt and loose top standing by his side with 4-5 books in her hand that she was unable to handle. Suddenly, the bus braked and the books tumbled down on him. She apologized, blushed with embarrassment, and Shekhar rose chivalrously. Initially, she declined but when Shekhar told her, "I don't want to undergo the same experience again," she smiled and accepted the offer.

It was the month of August, there was a gentle drizzle in the air. The bus raced to over sixty, her blouse fluttered in the breeze, and bending down he saw her fair breasts. Even the small black mole. His body grew tense; he had never seen such beautiful breasts from such close quarters. A few stops later, the elderly gentleman alighted and Shekhar sat down beside her. He introduced himself that he was in the final year, Chemistry (Honours), Hindu College.

"I am Shivani, Botany (Honours) first year, same college." She smiled brightly at him.

The next day she spotted him in the coffee house and spent more than two hours with him, bunking her classes. They grew fond of each other and talked and talked in the rain, the bright wintry afternoons, and under the starry skies. He got a position in the university, and joined M.Sc. He was already in love with her; she took another two years to realize it. Her parents were aware of their affair; he intended to inform his parents of his plan to marry Shivani after getting selected in civil services. While window – shopping at Karolbagh, she selected the trousseau for her marriage, decided the number of children they will have, their names and even chartered their careers.

A radiant moon thrilled Shivani, and a sad moon upset her. She associated a pale, yellow moon with unhappiness and suffering. Once she confided in Shekhar, "My grandma believes that a red moon heralds death. And I have seen it happen many times in our family." His logical arguments were unable to allay her fears.

When he learnt of his selection in the Indian Revenue Service, they were jubilant. In that fit of euphoria, he brought Shivani to his rented flat on the terrace at Model Town and made love to her. They were not sure whether he was able to penetrate her or not but they both enjoyed the unique experience. "God is blessing us," she whispered looking up at the marbled sky. The next time he wanted to do it, she said, "Let us get married, first."

Shekhar introduced Shivani to his parents, who resided at Meerut. His father rejected the marriage alliance though his mother was floored by Shivani's beauty. His father needed tons of money for the marriage of three daughters and was aware that Shivani's parents from lower middle class strata of society could not afford; this aspect, however, was not discussed. Shekhar argued fiercely, he loved her, and did not want to desert her.

"How could you think of marrying her?" His father roared at him. "Who will marry your sisters if you marry a non Aggarwal girl?"

A Brahmin, Shivani Tewari could not be inducted in an Aggarwal household. Shekhar did not have the spine to stand up to his father; he owed him a lot for spending his hard earned money on his education. Shekhar buckled under pressure, and gave in. Shivani was shattered.

Shekhar, Shivani met for the last time at Standard, their favourite rendezvous. In protest, she had taken the seat opposite him. With tears streaming down her cheeks, Shivani said, "I feared it all along; it was too good to be true." Shekhar apologized that he could not go against his father, and she went on ranting it was all her fault. She did not touch the cutlets and cake slices, and refused even to take tea. He wanted to move over to her sofa to assuage her feelings, she forbade him to do so.

"It's the last time we are seeing each other," she told him coldly, and abruptly rose. "Don't ever try to see me again."

She walked away from his life without looking back at him.

Shekhar's father selected Ruchira; her father was prepared to meet all his demands. It was Shekhar's good fortune that Ruchira was pleasant and amiable. In fact, physically, she was the opposite of Shivani. Ruchira was skinny, short, dark, and almost flat. She loved him, and was turned on by his very touch.

His PA reminded him twice about the meeting at 3pm, but he was lost in the past and forgot about it. He rushed to the conference room and found his boss and Director General, Narcotics waiting for him. Laxmi Subramanian, his boss, frowned perceptibly at his late arrival. DG, Narcotics explained that Satish Verma, the underworld don, was trying to smuggle narcotics worth about fifty million dollars in the next one or two weeks. Central Bureau Investigations (CBI) was also being co-opted. The modality of the operation and its strategy was discussed. Shekhar was to spearhead the operation, and was directed to position his trusted men in key positions.

It was past five when the meeting was over. He had a message passed on to his wife that he would be late.

Shekhar contemplated the restaurant; he had never visited the place again after their break up. Nothing seemed to have changed. The old furniture, the discoloured upholstery, the faded curtains, the waiters with prominent frowns and lackadaisical gait appeared to move in the same beaten track for last two decades: the atmosphere looked insipid and dull. A feeling of ennui swept over him. In those days when he was with Shivani, the world, suffused in their love, was vibrant, and gilded with a touch of heady spring. Shekhar's eyes turned misty. He sipped his coke thoughtfully, looked down below at the traffic on the Connaught Circus and wondered what did Shivani want from him after all these years?

He saw Shivani enter the hall and walk directly to his corner seat. Dressed in a starched white sari turned yellow with years, she looked gaunt; the skin around her face was tighter and the nose once sharp, appeared askew on her delicate face. She looked faded like her sari. She wore no jewellery and no make- up. Shekhar was not happy to see her. He had expected the old Shivani to spring out of the door and flaunt her azure smiles at him. He rose from his seat with a warm 'hello' and wanted to take her hands, but she folded them in a namaste. Slightly put off, he just managed to smile.

"How have you been all these years, Shivani?" He asked affectionately looking at her sad, liquid eyes.

"Not too well," she answered, and sat down on the sofa opposite him and looked minutely at him. In a blue Arrow shirt, soft coloured Park Avenue trousers, Omega gold watch, sparkling golden chain, bursting tummy, and a prominent double chin, Shekhar gave loud signals of being rich and satisfied with life.

"You look prosperous." She commented, and noticed that he had a darker tan than before.

Not liking her comment, he smiled wryly. "I am a survivor."

The waiter brought a soft drink for her. She inquired about the family.

"Ruchi is fine, and busy in her kitty parties." His elder son was in Roorkee Engineering College, and the younger one had just moved to eleventh class.

When he asked her about the family she burst into tears. "I lost my husband two years back. He committed suicide."

"What?" His voice turned hoarse. She nodded.

He wanted to move over to her seat, wipe the tears and pacify her; she stopped him with a sign of her hand.

"I am sorry," he said, and shook his head. "And your children?"

She sobbed for a while, and he watched her helplessly as he had done the last time they had met. Regaining her composure, she told him her story.

Satyadev Dubey, her husband, had been the vice principal of Happy Valley School, Lucknow and was hoping to be the principal shortly. Inderdev, their only son, was a worthless student. With lot of pull they arranged a clerical job for him in Punjab and Sind Bank. In two years, he swindled fifteen lakhs from the bank and left the country; his whereabouts were not known to anyone including the police. The Dubeys belonged to a small village near Lucknow; they were not rich, but their name was taken with respect and dignity as they stood for traditions and old values. The only market and road junction was named after their peers. Satyadev could not stand the snide comments of his village folk and committed suicide. The police was harassing her to return the money. To restore the dignity and honour of the family she had decided to pay back the money taken by her son. She sold everything she had, and was still short of five lakhs.

"I want your help Shekhar. I have tried everywhere but drawn a blank. I need five lakhs."

"I'll try Shivani," he said, his voice lacked in confidence. His house was under construction and he was running out of money. He had borrowed heavily from government, and financial institutions, and more than 50% of his pay was being deducted. His son wanted to join Akash Coaching institution, and he needed another Rs 1 lakh. Unfortunately for him, because of his new boss, his sources of extra income had dried up. If Shivani had asked this money last year, he could have given it readily.

"I could never imagine even in my wildest dreams that my own son would act in such a disgraceful manner. Remember the lofty ideas we discussed in the campus and the idealism we shared."

"That was in the past, Shivani." He fidgeted nervously. "We all change with times."

When the waiter brought cutlets and cake slices, she smiled for the first time. "You have not forgotten those times."

How could he have forgotten the days he had spent with her? Controlling himself, he shook his head slightly. His throat was choked and he concentrated on his cutlets, his eyes glued to the plate.

She prepared the tea; it was her prerogative.

He raised his eyes and looked at her. Her once lustrous hair had streaks of grey, the shapely arms he had fondled in the past so often were thin and lacked in sensuality; the lips he had kissed passionately were shapeless, as if they had not been touched for decades. She had lost her youth much before her years, he reflected. He held himself responsible for it.

Sipping tea, he said, "You must be very lonely in life, Shivani."
"We all have to live with our loneliness, Shekhar."

The sharpness in her tone hurt him.

She gazed downwards at the traffic, remembered something and smiled. "Remember, once we had to run across the road –"

Shekhar nodded. A bus moving at a great speed from Parliament Street had taken them by surprise and they ran across the road otherwise they would have been crushed under the vehicle. It was her fault but she had held him responsible for it. That was the day he had kissed her the first time.

Shaking her head, she dismissed the past.

When he had finished tea, she told him not to escort her as some of her relatives had to meet her at Regal. She gave him her contact number. He told her that he would need about a week to arrange for money.

"And I am depending upon you Shekhar." She rose from her seat and turning, walked towards the door, her carriage firm and straight.

He sat down, and ordered another pot of tea.

"Five lakhs," he muttered staring at the seat opposite as if Shivani was still sitting there. He tried to remember the withered face of the new Shivani he had met, the old images superimposed themselves. The new Shivani was not real. She was not his Shivani, but the wife of Satyadev Dubey who also was not real. He was dead. But he had been honest!

Marriage had changed Shekhar's attitude to life. Ruchira was given to a sybaritic life style, and she believed that marrying a Custom and Excise officer was the key to cornucopia of riches. Fond of diamonds, expensive silk saris, and travelling abroad, she forced her husband to take bribes. In the beginning, he was scared, gradually became bolder and later, reckless. Ruchira saw a plot at Noida, was bowled over and told her husband to buy it. Shekhar wavered; Ruchira retaliated by going on hunger fast and did not talk to him for a week. Coerced by her conduct, Shekhar yielded, purchased the plot and paid a heavy price. He was involved in a vigilance case, and served a major charge sheet. The case dragged on for many years and though bribery was not established, he was given a minor punishment for flouting prescribed procedure and lost out on promotion. Officers two years his junior superseded him. It did not chastise him, and he continued getting his cut in the Excise wing. Fortunately, he did not get caught. Two years back he was transferred to Custom and was comfortably getting his monthly commission. Laxmi Subramanian's taking over as Collector changed the scenario, as she was scrupulously honest. Aware of his past track record, she did not trust him.

In a meeting with the revenue officers last month, the new Central Vigilance Commissioner had warned of dire consequences if high standards of morality were not maintained. Shekhar, with a tainted past, had to watch his step.

And now another five lakhs were required for Shivani! He expected his promotion in six months; any slip could be suicidal for him. If he had married Shivani, life would have been so different, he thought.

At night, Shekhar glanced at his wife as she picked up the phone in her nightdress, and gossiped with her younger sister. It came as a rude shock to him that pampered by comforts, and luxuries, now she looked beautiful and had much more sex appeal than Shivani.

Next day, he was unable to concentrate at his work. Shekhar took out a piece of paper and switched on the red light. It was his habit since last many years to parse his problems, personal and official by scribbling on paper. He wrote: 1. Shivani's son misappropriated the money. 2. Her son was corrupt. 3. Shivani needs five lakhs. 4 Shivani's husband & family were honest.

Collector's PA called to inform that the Chief had sent for him. Whenever she was not happy with him, which was often, the message came through her PA. He locked the sheet in the locker and went to his boss.

Shekhar dreaded her sharp comments. Confident of her political connections through her husband who hobnobbed with the Cabinet Ministers, she did not spare the Board Members with her tongue-in- cheek repartees. Attired in a red sari, a scowl on her face, she raised a number of issues in which he had not given the feedback. Without a comment, he jotted down the points. For an instant, his mind wandered back to Shivani. He admonished himself and jerked his head slightly to concentrate on the instructions of the boss.

"Isn't Ruchi allowing you to sleep properly?" She spoke harshly. "I want a report on all these within three days."

"I will try," he said stiffly and left the room.

He unlocked his drawer, took out the sheet and wrote: 5. But I am corrupt???. He stared at the sheet for a long time, suddenly called his driver, and decided to see his father at Meerut.

Shekhar picked up his father from the confectionery shop located at the main crossing opposite the Railway Station, and drove down to his ancestral house. He knew his father was thrilled with pride whenever he sat in the official car. He spent an hour with his old parents, however, could not muster the courage to ask for loan.

On return, he stopped at Police Head Quarters near ITO and called upon Parmjeet Singh, his batch mate and asked him for money. Paramjeet was going through a lean patch as he was fighting a property litigation case against his brother, and could not spare any money.

In the morning, he visited North Block, which houses the offices of Ministry of Finance and the Board of Indirect Taxes.

He met some of his friends and asked for loan. Vaneet, a smooth operator who had made millions and had never been caught, said, "It's like King Solomon begging for alms." Shekhar's tarnished image haunted him everywhere. He spent the whole day moving from seat to seat hoping something would turn up. Though the mission was a failure, the grape vine was full of rumours that Shekhar needed money.

After 4-5 days, his boss called him and directly questioned him about the gossip circulating in North Block. Blatantly, he denied it. "It's the handiwork of my enemies," he said.

Her face stolidly grim, her piercing eyes boring into his, she said threateningly, "If you indulge in any hanky- panky, it is the black hole for you, Shekhar! Am I clear?"

The whining of the AC was loud and unpleasant.

"Is there anything else?" The hostility in his voice did not go unnoticed by her. With a shake of her head, she dismissed him.

Smarting from the insult, he had just entered his room when Shivani called.

"Oh, yes, Shivani?" He asked for some more time, as he was unable to arrange for the money.

"Can you make it fast Shekhar? It is really getting difficult for me."

The panic in her tone gave him goose pimples.

"I am trying -- "

But she had switched off. He tried her number repeatedly and was not able to reach her. She must be at the breaking point otherwise she wouldn't behave in this manner.

He was restless at night. Left with no option, he told his wife about Shivani. How he had met, loved and promised to marry her and was forced to let her down. He told her sad story and the need for money to save her honour. He wanted her to sell 3-4 pieces of diamond jewellery or take the money from her brother who had a flourishing practice in the High Court. Ruchira was stunned. At the eve of her marriage, she had vaguely heard of a Shivani from her mother- in- law and had dismissed her from her thoughts, as she was confident of her father's riches and the love she had for Shekhar. Her reappearance after so many years and Shekhar's getting upset on her account made her uneasy. Ruchira bluntly refused to permit her husband to give money to Shivani. He patiently explained that he had left her in lurch once and did not want to do it again for he cared for her.

"I would rather use the money for my house," she screamed at him making her stand clear. One argument led to the other, and they both shouted at each other.

"What the hell do I care about her honour? Let the bitch go to jail — that's what she richly deserves."

"Shut up!" He slapped her hard. "Do you know that it is you and I who deserve to go to jail for having swindled the govt. funds?"

For the first time in his marital life, he slept in the drawing room.

How could he tell Ruchira that he still loved Shivani?

It was a night of turmoil. Suddenly, he peeped out of the window and looked at the heavens. The moon was a pale yellow. A shiver ran down his spine when he remembered that Shivani associated the yellow moon with misfortune.

Full of determination, he sent for Surinder Seth, Superintendent, Custom, as soon as he reached the office next day. Seth was the conduit who had links with the underworld. Shekhar looked minutely at him, and whispered, "Let us go in for the big kill." Seth was surprised for no one dared to risk one's future in an operation of this nature when the premier investigating agencies were directly keeping a watch. The Deputy Collector must be desperate, he concluded. Seth confided that Verma's men had approached him, but he had not committed. They discussed the nitty-- gritty of the case: double- crossing their own men, positioning of the Collector's trusted men in insignificant areas and cuts at various levels due to increased risk. Shekhar got a message from PA to the boss that she wanted to see him. He took his own time and thrashed out all the facets of the counter operation once again with Seth. When Shekhar rose from his chair Seth warned him. "Sir, beware of the old fox."

"I'll handle her," he said.

Shekhar reached the Chief's room after twenty minutes. Seated on the revolving chair and facing the map of the airport pinned on the wall, her back towards the door, she was busy talking on the phone. "I have warned him personally," he heard her boisterous voice. "If I smell his involvement even remotely, I'll screw his balls so hard that he will forget about his promotion till his retirement."

Shekhar withdrew discretely and learnt from her PA that she was in conversation with Senior Deputy Director, CBI.

He realized he had reached the cul-de-sac. Now, the die was cast.

Fifteen minutes later he went to the Collector's room, and the two finalized the strategy in Verma's case. She told him that she had spoken to Senior Deputy Director, CBI.

"I had a word with the Assistant Director, CBI in the morning," he told her. With a poker face, Shekhar briefed her on the specific areas where help of CBI was being sought.

For once, she was duped. Maybe the rumours were absurd, she thought.

At the kitty party, Ruchira overheard the story about Shekhar's visit to North Block and confronted him directly on his return from the office. She was sarcastic with him for going around with a begging bowl on behalf of his ex- girl friend. Not getting any reaction from him infuriated her, and she threatened him. "Shekhar, if you do anything stupid, you will lose me."

Unmoved, he went to the bedroom and closed the door, his mind racing through the issues he had discussed with Seth.

For the next few days, the office buzzed with excitement and feverish activity, although no one mentioned the name of don Satish Verma; it was supposed to be top secret. The weekend was going to be worse for the consignment was expected on Saturday night or early hours of Sunday.

On Friday, he felt so edgy that he left the office abruptly lest his behaviour gave him away. He had handled similar operations in the past with aplomb, today his hands were clammy and he startled on screeching of a chair.

Ruchira went out of the way to be sweet to him. Something was cooking in the office, she could sense it from her husband's conduct, but he refused to share it with her. Neither could she elicit any information from Shekhar's colleagues. The vertical lines appearing on his forehead were a matter of grave concern, she had seen them only on the day he had received the charge sheet. The number of mobile calls had increased over the last 2-3 days and he switched on the mobile only in the bedroom. Over a cup of tea, she talked on disparate topics without expecting any response from him. He finished his cup and stood on the balcony.

With temperature soaring to 44 degrees Celsius, there was no reprieve for the Delhites from the hot winds lashing Delhi since afternoon.

Ruchira walked over to him and placed her arm around him.

"Please, Shekhar, tell me what is happening in the office?" He did not make any remark and neither reciprocated her warmth.

"You may not tell me but I can feel something serious is brewing." She caught his hand. "Whatever it be, for god's sake do not jeopardize the future of our children. And I know you love them as much as I do."

She pressed his hand gently. He saw her eyes were full of tears. Abruptly, she left him and went to the kitchen.

From the balcony, he saw many boys competing at the high jump in the newly developed park. A small boy, much younger than others, tried to jump the bar and could not make it. The bar hit his body and he was slightly hurt. He took another chance but when he reached the bar again, his legs froze. A loud boo rose from the boys. The seniors were wild at him. "Go and hide in your mama's lap," they shouted. However the boy was stubborn. With determination, he ran again and with a big leap crossed the bar. There was a resounding applause from everyone including the residents at their balconies. Shekhar gave a loud cheer and was moved by the heroic effort of the youngster.

The boy did not get up to acknowledge the accolades and others rushed and lifted him.

When Ravi, his son, appeared at dinnertime, Shekhar asked about the incident at the playground. "Oh, Vinod, the stupid fool!" He spoke about him in disparaging terms. An 8th class student, he was trying to compete with 11th and 12th class boys. "Just because he was ridiculed by some of us, he tried to jump such a high bar much higher than his puny size." Ravi added. Vinod was seriously hurt and taken to Ram Manohar Lohia Hospital. Ruchira spoke to Vinod's mother in details. Later, she informed Shekhar that the boy was to be operated upon. "It is possible that he may lose his left leg."

"Shit," Ravi said dramatically. "The stupid fool - he was trying to overreach himself - he had to fall."

Shekhar left the table without taking his dessert.

Ruchira was right. Vinod lost his leg in an emergency operation carried out on Saturday morning.

Shekhar was grave and irritable throughout the day. Nervously, he clutched at his mobile, listened, gave directions and often lost his temper. He had pulled down shutters of silence on the face of his wife though he played chess with his son for sometime in the afternoon. In the evening, he went for a long drive all by himself mulling over the situation. The words of his son discomforted him.

On return, he told his wife to close all the doors and windows as a dust storm was expected.

At eleven in the night, he switched on the mobile. "Seth, operation 'old fox' is off."

"It is too late, boss. I can't withdraw."

"Obey my orders." His voice was menacing. "If you go ahead, it is your funeral."

And he switched off the mobile.

He opened the door to the balcony. The sky was covered with a yellow hue; the dust storm was expected to break any moment. He turned his head towards the east and saw the pale red moon. Ghoulishly frightening. A wave of fear swept over him, and he quivered. "I have let you down again, Shivani," he muttered, and collapsed in the chair.

And he wept.

Ruchira, who was watching him like a shadow, threw her arms around him.

■■■

Spin in the Rain

Narendra Chopra looked down from the window of the Boeing and saw a sea of white clouds floating leisurely. As a small child, he wanted to reach up to the clouds, explore their unknown mystery, touch them and whisper to them how he felt about the world around him. Today, he was at a higher altitude than the clouds. A senior Director in the Ministry of Finance, he was likely to be promoted as Joint Secretary in next one or two months. At 39, he felt he was on the top of the world. He was on a special mission to Patna for a week to inquire into improper utilization of funds allotted by the Centre to the state of Bihar. The Comptroller Auditor General had passed strictures in the annual report and the Chairperson, Public Accounts Committee, had desired an inquiry.

Naren was given a warm reception by the State Government officials and was escorted to the guest house of Controller, Defence Accounts as the Circuit House was in repairs. During office hours, he familiarized himself with the details of the case. In the evening, the State Government officials hosted a dinner and officers of both Central and State governments were introduced to him.

He was about to leave for office in the morning when someone said, "Morning, sir." He looked up and noticed a tall, smart girl dressed in a thick black top and off white jeans smiling at him. She had typical Tamilian features -- wide luminous eyes, full lips, sharp nose, a flawless light olive complexion and long hair. "I am Shailja Srinivasan." She smiled. "We met yesterday in the party."

She was also staying at the guest house.

"Oh, yes, yes." He recalled she was wearing a dark green sari that made her look darker. She had hardly registered on him for there were a number of pretty lady officers and wives of other officers around. Looking at his watch, he told her he was getting late and would see her in the evening.

It was the month of July. The grey, dark clouds that had been threatening since morning burst into heavy rain in the evening. When he reached the guest house, he threw the briefcase on the bed and ascended the steps to the terrace from the side corridor. Standing in the doorway, his attention was riveted to the other end of the long terrace. A girl was spinning on her toes. Her hands were stretched wide, face pointing to the heavens, eyes closed, hair clinging to her face and neck as the rain lashed down on her. Her movement was lyrical, as she swung round like a child in ecstasy. Mesmerized by her rhythmic body movement, his eyes followed her as she moved towards his end of the terrace. All of a sudden, he remembered that the girl was dressed in the same top and jeans that Shailja had been wearing in the morning.

Despite the torrential rain, the dark clouds scattered in the far off western hemisphere, and a bright golden hue splashed across the sky like a semi ellipse tapering off to a deep crimson. It was as if the gates of heaven had been thrown open. The simmering golden yellow light of the setting sun suffused her mustard face and she looked divine. Her twirling increased to a crescendo, as if she was unable to control her wild joy. The faster she whirled, the happier she seemed. She was so close to the boundary wall that he was about to run up to her, but realised she was not unaware of her surroundings.

Hastily, he withdrew and hid behind the door as she speedily moved across to his side. The sky, which had turned saffron, was in the backdrop like a painting. She was like a dancer dancing to the tune of the rain pouring down from heaven. The lightning flashed, the clouds thundered. Swept by seraphic joy, her rotation grew faster, as if she was dancing to the beat of the `nagara'.

Naren wanted to reach out and join her. But he also did not wish to invade her privacy and spoil the scene that had impregnated his heart. He tiptoed back to his room.

His first memory of clouds was at Shimla where he spent the first eight years of his childhood. The clouds entered the house and he felt the mist and liked it. Down below, in the valleys, he saw the clouds resting peacefully. Sometimes, they raced away faster than even his thoughts.

A lonely child, he fantasized that the clouds were angels and dragons at war with one another. At times, he spun his own stories around them and himself became the hero, rescuing pretty damsels, performing heroic deeds. It was different in Delhi. When the first drops of rain fell on the muddy earth, a heady smell filled the atmosphere. He liked it. He would strip and dash into the rain. The harder the rain struck his body, the more ecstatic he felt. Swept by frenzy, he ran around and frolicked like a wild animal, all by himself. However, marriage had changed him.

For Asha, his wife, felt it was downright vulgarity to get drenched in the rain and unwillingly, he had acquiesced to her way of thinking. She was exceedingly proper in her manners, conduct and general behaviour. No one could fault her for the lack of control over emotions. Not even in the privacy of her bedroom. Her smiles, expressions, tone and body language were impeccable. She was almost like a machine. In her attitude to the children, she was exactly a copy of her mother, a strict disciplinarian.

She dutifully embraced her husband and the children when she met them outside the home. Within the four walls, she did not approve of physical intimacy, especially with the children. "It spoils them," she told him. Perhaps, she felt the same way about him too.

She never let herself go. She never opened up, except her legs for the sexual act. But she never participated in it either. She let him make love only so that he did not run to other women. Asha allowed him to play with her body, though sometimes he had the uncanny feeling that she saw his act objectively, from a distance, and perhaps considered it plebeian.

Maybe her needs were not the same as his, he had reflected. His mother had once remarked, "Isn't Asha rather cold?" He had dismissed it as the usual fault finding reaction of a mother- in- law. Naren had loved and worshipped Asha for years and he could not imagine that she was anything less than perfect.

Today, he was not as charitable to her. Her coldness hurt him though he did not allow it to be noticed by anyone. Naren had the genes of West Punjabis (his parents had migrated from Pakistan during the partition), who are full of warm bubbly emotions and do not make any pretence to control them.

And they love the rain. Even in winter. The cousins hugged, embraced, backslapped and exchanged abusive language. Asha dubbed them crude and gradually, he distanced himself from his cousins, though he missed their warmth and affection.

The caretaker knocked to inform that dinner was ready. Naren closed his book and walked over to the lounge- cum- dining room of the guest house. Shailja, couched in front of the television, was engrossed in a family serial. When he entered, she rose and wished him. He noticed a prominent bandage on one of her toes. She explained that she had slipped in the rain and looking at his worried face, added, "Nothing serious, sir."

"Do you like the rain?" he asked.

"Oh, I love it." Her face brightened. "We all do — my parents, brothers, and sisters. And my husband loves to frisk and fool around in the rain. What about you, Sir?"

"I just adore it," he spoke spontaneously.

Naren learnt she was in P&T Finance Accounts Service and had joined the office of the Chief General Manager, Telecommunication a month back. It was her first posting.

"I am in a mess," she said. "My husband is in Mumbai, my one– year–old daughter in Delhi with my parents and I am here." She talked of her husband, her daughter, and later spoke to both of them on phone. Naren watched her expressions. Her face flushed with excitement when she spoke to her hubby and her eyes turned moist as she talked to her mother and child. He found her to be a very warm, affectionate person and he enjoyed conversing with her.

Next evening, he reached the guest house rather late. It was almost dark. Shailja caught him in the lounge and informed him that the cook had to rush to his village as his father was on deathbed. The office was unable to make any alternative arrangement. They had no choice but to eat out. She was familiar with the city and escorted him to Chanakya, a short distance away. Naren liked the ambience of the restaurant. Over dinner, Shailja kept on talking about her husband, daughter and the office. She had a penchant for telling interesting stories about her office and would break into peals of laughter. Sometimes, she would close her eyes, her face pointing towards the ceiling and shake her fingers vigorously, unmindful that some noodles had fallen on her shirt.

He also told her about his beautiful wife, and how he had been crazy about her since school days. But she had noticed him only when he made it to the IAS. She was the rage of the university. He was successful in wooing her because of the casting vote of her bureaucratic father. Naren's name had been recommended for a World Bank assignment, a slot earmarked for India and he was likely to receive his orders shortly.

"Congratulations, sir." Shailja smiled at him. Later, narrating a story about the Chief General Manager, her laughter rang in the dining hall and many heads turned towards them, though she was not conscious of the tears streaming down her cheeks.

Naren was so charmed with her infectious laughter that he also laughed aloud like a college student, which would have been considered a sacrilege in his house. Everything about her was so intense and passionate that it was difficult for anyone to be untouched by it.

Out of the blue, she asked, "Did you see me in the rain yesterday?" Her hands on the table, her eyes looked expectantly at him. "Intuitively, I realized someone was looking at me."

He nodded.

"I had gone crazy, but I have never enjoyed myself so much in my own company." She confided in him as if it were a secret. Her liquid eyes sparkled and she looked devastatingly beautiful. It was the first time in his life that he found anyone to be as pretty as his wife. He wanted to touch Shailja on the bare arm and hold her hands but refrained from doing so.

They had their dinner and breakfast together and enjoyed each other's company. Sometimes, Naren consulted her on accounts matter and found her advice to be sound.

A week later, when both of them were busy trying to decipher a document and had just concluded that it was forged, the phone rang.

"Are you O.K?" Asha sounded worried.

It suddenly occurred to him that he had forgotten to call her up in the evening. He assured her everything was well; he had been busy going through the files, as he wanted to be back by Tuesday.

"Do you know the time? It is past ten. I have been waiting for your call for the last two hours!" Asha snapped. Shailja quietly slipped away to her room.

For the next two days, he worked tirelessly from morning till late night and was able to finish his work on Monday. He decided to leave by the five p.m. flight.

Unable to contact Shailja on phone, he decided to look her up in the office en route to airport. Knocking at her door, he entered and found her deep in discussion with an officer. There was no power and the room was not lighted adequately.

She rose abruptly and dismissed the officer. "I just came to say goodbye, Shailja," Naren said and offered his hand. She eagerly grasped it with both her hands.

The warmth that exuded from her hands and pervaded his body was a strange experience. Like a tsunami of joy, it bewildered him. He felt this touch was even more intimate than what he felt when he made love to his wife.

"I will miss you, sir," she said, her voice turning husky. "I had a great time with you."

"I will never forget you, Shailja," he mumbled and kissed her hand.

He caressed her cheeks for a long time and wanted to kiss her on the lips but bridled his rising emotions with superhuman effort.

He tore himself from her, and added, "Good bye, Shailja."

Asha and the kids were at the airport to receive him with a large bouquet of gladioli and roses. He kissed his children and tightly hugged his wife.

Suddenly, Shailja's beautiful face flashed across him, spinning, spinning in the rain silhouetted against a bright golden yellow sky.

■ ■ ■

Diamonds

It was one of those misty January nights when the cold seeps into the marrow of bones, and makes you shiver. The wind was icy and biting. Wrapped in our thick woollens from head to toe, Rati and I felt clumsy, and faltered on the steps in the dimly lit stairway, but our daughter Ragini ran up the three flights and rang the bell. Amit Ganguly opened the door, and welcomed us with all the warmth he was capable of, and he was capable of plenty. In fact, he excelled at it. He could make you feel that the world was a worthwhile place because of friends like him.

Amit had bought a flat in Noida about three months back. We could not attend the house warming party and he was annoyed. I have few friends and Rati did not want me to lose out on him. When Nisha, Amit's wife, invited us again with a NRI friend, and threatened 'If you don't come, I'll never invite you again,' we had braved the severe winter, apprehensive of the smog on the return journey.

It was a three-bedroom flat with a spacious drawing cum dining room glowing in white marble flooring, off white walls, and sky blue ceiling. Replicas of Picasso, Van Gogh, and Rembrandt adorned the walls; a medium sized chandelier of intricate design lit the room. The wrought iron furniture with contrasting deep blue cushions reflected the aesthetics of the mistress of the house. At the corners, white, yellow chrysanthemums in huge painted earthen vases added colour to the cosy room. The bedrooms were artistically done up with new furniture out of a showroom.

"You have blown a fortune." Rati commented uneasily trailing behind Nisha.

"All that we have," Nisha replied. "And we are neck deep in loans." Rati gave me a reproachful look as we had been searching for a flat for last two years, and were still indecisive because of the prohibitive costs.

"Why don't we buy a house like this, papa?" Ragini echoed her mother's sentiments. She knew that Amit, and I belong to Indian Revenue Service, and I was one year senior to him.

I smiled sheepishly.

"Your papa is a little stupid, and has limited vision." Amit shrugged his shoulders, and smiled.

Such banters were common between us with a friendship spanning more than a quarter of a century; Ragini accepted it without a comment.

Amit's smile was enigmatic and it confused me. Maybe, I could not understand my college friend, and sometimes it infuriated me. He had a supercilious air bordering on the condescending as though he was out to dupe the world. As Director (Vigilance), I had helped him twice when he was in deep trouble. Just before my promotion last year, at a slight risk to my own career, I had absolved him of a serious vigilance charge fully believing that he was innocent.

The deep bonding between Ragini and Amit's eldest daughter Priti had brought the two families close. Without a sibling, Ragini had a few kinks, and didn't gel easily with her class mates. We made sure that she and Priti did not miss out on any opportunity to be together.

For two hours we waited for the NRI friend, and his family. Amit refused to tell me the name of the person, and to add to my irascibility, assured that I knew him. My past experience with NRI friends had not been a pleasant one, and I was slightly skeptical. Rati frowned frequently, she was not happy that Ragini was wasting her time in useless gossip with her bosom friend instead of mugging her notes for Pre-Boards.

"I think we should make a move." I rose looking at my watch; it registered 10.45pm.

"How can you do it?" Nisha walked over to me, and forced me back on my seat. The mobile rang; the NRI guest had lost his way. Amit gave the directions, and was promised they would be there in next five minutes.

After half an hour, the bell rang and Amit rushed to open the door. I could not have recognised Satish Aggarwal if I had run into him anywhere else. Casually dressed in shabby jeans, a close fitting pullover with a collar, hideous feet exposed in bathroom slippers, and an unshaven face, Satish projected a pretentious intellectual air though to me he seemed uncouth. Often, he wrapped his arms around his chest as if protecting himself from the worst of Delhi winter. Rati had forced me to wear my best three- piece suit, and I felt embarrassed. Satish planned to be in Delhi for next 8-9 weeks, and had brought half a dozen of his close relatives with whom he was staying. Later, I gathered from Amit that Satish was a professor at Columbia University.

Since it was unusually late, we all attacked the food as soon the introductions were over.

"Arvind Sahani," Satish said and looked at me thrusting a spoonful of rice in his mouth, his eyes luminous. "I can never forget you. You were the one who stole Parminder's watch, and were dubbed as the most infamous thief of Hindu College." He continued to berate me.

"It wasn't Arvind, it was someone else." Amit intervened half-heartedly.

"Who?" Satish laughed.

I was paralysed. The over squeamish Rati looked coldly at me, and stopped eating. Nausea swept over Ragini, and she rushed to the washroom. Her childhood hero was besmirched. Satish continued to ridicule me. Pushed to the wall I do not react, my hands grow clammy, and my senses go numb.

"Stop insulting my guest," Nisha shouted. "I know Arvind for years. He can never do such a thing."

Satish persisted. "It was the talk of the college in those days."
"Oh, shut up!" Nisha snubbed him again.

Dishonoured, I was in no position to raise my eyes. I wondered why Amit had invited me along with Satish. "Ragini has to take her Pre-Boards day after," Rati said firmly, and was on her feet. Ragini and I followed her though Nisha protested that we had not touched the dessert.

As soon as the door closed behind us and we descended the stairs, we heard muffled laughter. Amit saw us off. "I am sorry," he muttered, and waved his hand.

No one exchanged a word till we reached home. Ragini dashed to her room, and banged it shut.

Once the bedroom door was bolted, Rati exploded. "For twenty years I have been tolerating this holier than thou image! The most upright officer in the organization! For years, I have been keeping the vouchers of the various buys so that no mala fide is associated to you. We have never taken any concessions. No perks and facilities from any damn person. You have never bought me a single piece of jewellery since our marriage. And look at your friend — a new three-bedroom flat, a new car, new furniture, AC in the bedroom. And today I learn that you were a thief in your college days, and that too a famous one!"

Tears ran down her cheeks. "What the hell have I got out of life? The most notorious student of Hindu college as my husband!"

"Will you judge me based on remarks made by an old class fellow? Give me a chance to explain. My explanation will convince you that I am innocent."

"It better be a good one." She continued in the same high pitch.

"Give me five minutes," I said, and disappeared in the washroom.

I took a long time; it worried Rati, and she knocked twice.

When I emerged, she pounced on me. "Shoot, I want to know everything."

I was the hero of Hindu college. The captain of the cricket team, and the best batsman the college had produced in last two decades. I had helped the college win the inter-college championship for three years in a row, and was tipped for Delhi Ranji Trophy team. Boys and girls adulated me. I could silence the unruly students with a mere gesture of my hands.

When I was in MA (Previous), Raj Kumar, and Satish Aggarwal joined our hostel. Both were bowlers, and wanted a place in the cricket team. In the selection trials, Amit, my room-mate was dropped, Satish could not make it, and Raj Kumar was selected. Amit and Satish harboured a common grouse against me; I could not help it. Amit continued to share my room, and was my buddy all the twenty-four hours as before.

Parminder, my neighbour, was a rich businessman's son; his sisters visited him frequently. Someone stole his sister's Omega diamond watch, and the rumour in the college and hostel corridors was that Raj Kumar was the culprit. Raj Kumar belonged to a well-to-do farmer family, and appeared too decent to indulge in such a crime. No one believed the corridor gossip, however, someone was persistent in spreading it.

Walking in the hostel cloister at night, Amit and I discussed Raj Kumar, and felt his image was being tarnished unnecessarily. I was agitated, and said, "Raj Kumar is too simple and has pocketed the insult. If someone had dared it with us we would have taught the bastard a lesson." Amit was high and kept on chanting it like a nursery rhyme in the dead of the night, and I found it difficult to control him. I had to seek help of some friends to take him to the room.

Next day the rumour had taken a different colour. Now, I was blamed for stealing the diamond watch, eponymously called Parminder's watch. Initially, I ignored it. But it was on the notice board, in the classrooms, on the walls of the hostel and even in the toilets. The swashbuckling Arvind (that's me!) was shown hitting a six, and sporting a prominent diamond watch on his left hand. The caption read, 'the diamond watch thief hitting a six'.

I was shocked. It could not be happening to me, the cynosure of college. Someone was systematically maligning my image, and I could not fight him. The enemy was unknown. If I entered the class, a silence descended. No one sat on my bench. Even Amit was cold. In the college café or in the coffee house, if I walked towards a table, everyone left abruptly, and I had to gulp down coffee alone. My very presence was sufficient to break up a group. Such a thing had not happened in case of Raj Kumar: he was not famous. The college authorities decided to act and a search party was sent in the hostel. Nothing was found in our room or any other room. An inquiry committee was set up, and I was subjected to embarrassing questions - my father's income, the money received by me, the amount spent and so on. I felt humiliated, and met the principal.

He was all sympathy, however, showed his inability to intervene; it was a question of honour of college. The inquiry report exonerated me, and still there was no change in the attitude of my former friends or college students.

One day when I opened the drawer, I was stunned to see the diamond watch. Befuddled, I did not have the courage to even touch it. I scooted out of the room, and searched for Amit; I could not trace him. When I returned to the room, the watch was nowhere. I told Amit, he laughed it away. "You are having hallucinations."

It was the last straw.

I was not a fighter, I surrendered rather meekly. I left the hostel, and rented a room at Shaktinagar. Before I left, the authorities had planned another raid that somehow did not materialise.

Though I captained the college cricket team, we fared so poorly that we lost in the quarter- finals. Worse followed; I flunked in Previous.

Amit was the only one who interacted with me. He was warm and affectionate as before, but in presence of other college students he refused to show his friendliness. I understood, and did not blame him.

I had planned to go in for academics but the apocalyptic incident changed the course of my life. I took the civil services examination, and joined the Income Tax Service. Amit joined a year later.

"This is all I have to say," I said. "Do you believe me or not?"

Without replying, Rati switched off the lights.

Music filtering through the closed door of Ragini reminded me that I had another duty to perform. I knocked, and entered. The CD player was on, and Ragini was dancing. Whenever upset, she unwound herself in this way.

"I am having a break," she said lowering the volume. Her face was tense as if it would snap any moment.

"Would you like some coffee?" I suggested. I was aware she liked it when under stress.

She nodded. "I'll make it," she said, and left without waiting for my approval.

I looked at her physics notes, and found them smudged. I felt guiltier in presence of my daughter than my wife. If a grown up woman could not understand, how did I expect a teenager to appreciate my predicament?

Ragini brought the small cups of coffee she had presented us on our marriage anniversary.

"Yes, papa." She looked at me like an adult, more composed than her mother.

"My child, I want to talk to you — about what happened at the dinner," I said nervously. Surprisingly, I had been sure of myself with Rati.

Ragini nodded.

I repeated what I had told Rati. "I have told the same thing to your mama also."

"You have rehearsed it well," she replied in a metallic tone. It gave me goose pimples at four in the morning.

I was apprehensive that handling of my stubborn daughter would be more difficult, nonetheless, I had not bargained for the ruthlessness of her chilling remark.

Suddenly, I was deadbeat. I rose slowly, and turned. "Good night, papa." Her tone continued to be hostile.

I could not take it. I did not respond, and closed the door gently.

When I left for the office next day, my wife, and daughter were still sleeping. It was a new experience for me. For the last many years, Rati had always made sure that she gave me the breakfast, and the lunch pack. The feverish activity in the office made me forget my personal problems till I was on my way back home. I ruminated through the incidents of the previous night at the party, and my heart sank.

Rati opened the door without a smile. Her puffed eyes, tangled hair and haggard look indicated she was suffering from acute physical and mental pain. She called the maid who dutifully brought the tea tray, and left.

"What's up?" I asked trying to sound my usual self.

She did not react, looked at her watch, and informed me formally that she had to go to Mita's, our neighbour.

"Can't it wait?" I pleaded.

"No, it can't," she replied, and left.

Ragini walked into the drawing room, and suddenly stopped on seeing me. "Oh!" She gasped.

"Hello! How was the day?"

"OK, papa." She ran back to her room, and softly closed it.

I sensed that history was being repeated after twenty- four years. Except that it was not in the precincts of Hindu College, and the players were my wife, and my own blood. I could never dream that events of the past could affect my present in such a way. I realised I was facing a second Armageddon, it could be much worse than the last one. It could break me, and my family.

Rati returned at dinnertime, and we all sat down at the table. I talked of some funny incident that had actually occurred two weeks back making it up as if it had taken place that day. Neither of them laughed or smiled, their lips were sealed. Frustrated, I gave up after sometime, and left the dinner table.

I again explained to my wife that I had not stolen the watch, and was a victim of circumstances. She refused to believe me, and glared at me. "I have always been so proud of your honesty and integrity. And today I realised that you were branded a thief in the college, one who was forced to leave the hostel."

I had consciously avoided telling her that some of the ringleaders of the hostel had actually wanted me thrown out of the hostel. Lest the college authorities were forced to take such an extreme measure under pressure from the students union, I had taken the pre-emptive step, and quit the hostel.

Rati's reflexes were predictable. Daughter of a Session Judge, her standards of probity were high. It was not only a way of life with her but her religion too. She felt extremely proud that I, her husband, was equally scrupulous. Informally, I was told that in the column relating to integrity in the confidential reports, I was always graded `Impeccable'. In a party, a Member of the Board of Direct Taxes had once casually mentioned of it to Rati. It was saying a lot in our organisation. Our faces had suffused with pride, whereas those of many other officers including Amit (facing a vigilance case) had turned sheepish. We treasured such compliments, and it amply made up for luxuries we had denied ourselves.

"It is something that has happened, no one can undo it." I reminded her. "And it wasn't my fault."

"Then who stole the watch? Satish, Amit, Raj Kumar or someone else?"

"I don't know." I replied. "But definitely not Amit."

"You have to find out?" she said aloud. "I can't be having a normal relationship with a thief."

Rati was given to being illogical as she relied heavily on her intuition.

"My gut feeling is that you stole it," she said looking deep into my pale brown eyes, trying to fathom the truth as they did it to criminals, "otherwise you would have defended yourself yesterday."

Not getting any response from me, she reclined her head back on the pillow as if her premonitions had proved right. "But no, you sat like a Buddha — immune to the tongue lashing of Satish. And no one defended you — not even Amit."

She again looked at me. "Incidentally, I went to Amit's office today, and spent more than two hours with him. Though he swears by your friendship, he does not exonerate you. And he was present when the drama was being enacted." She winced, and glared at me. "Sometimes I feel I really don't know you at all. You are a total stranger to me."

She dismissed me by declaring that she wanted to sleep, and without waiting for any signal from me switched off the light. I was about to leave the room when she again clicked the switch, and said, "Now I know why Sneh left you."

I had told Rati about my first love, and her abandoning me but I had discreetly not confided about her reasons of desertion. It upset me that my own friend had leaked all the secrets of my life. Unable to contain my rising temper, I called Amit, and fired salvos of bitterness as to why he had not informed me about meeting with Rati. "She told me not to," was his short, crisp reply.

"What have you been telling her that she refuses to trust me?" "The truth, and nothing but the truth!"

"What was the need of talking about Sneh?" I thundered at him dubbing him a traitor.

"I could not stand her tears and told all I knew. You should have briefed me properly as to how much of your dirty linen is to be washed in front of Rati." He shouted back at me.

"You are a liar. How could Rati weep before you?" I yelled at him.

"It is a fact. She is cracking up; you need to take care of her." He kept on sermonizing that I should maintain my cool otherwise my family would break up. "It is an hour of crisis. I wish I could come over and talk to both of you, but I have no time as I am flying to States day after."

Four months back he had gone on deputation to Finance Ministry, and it was his first trip abroad. I had entirely forgotten about it. When I switched off the mobile I found my daughter looking hard at me; it appeared that she had been listening for some time. She ignored me, and walked over to her mother's room.

Sneh had left me on ethical grounds. She could not stand the daily chanting of `Arvind is a thief' in the college campus, and sent me a letter that she would not meet me again. It shattered me, but I could fall back on the support of my parents, and my sister.

Now, I had no one. My parents had died in a car accident, and my sister had settled in UK. She had divorced her husband, married an Englishman, and had sheared off herself from her roots and broken contact with me. Rati was my emotional anchor for last many years.

Next day, I went to Amit's office. He had gone to Air India office as some problem had arisen about his reservations. I waited for about an hour, and returned disappointed. I was not able to concentrate in my work, and cut a sorry figure in a meeting. When I reached home I faced the hostile stares of my wife and daughter. Lack of communication reigned at dinnertime. Only the passing of vegetable bowls, "Thanks," and the clatter of steel cutlery broke the offending silence.

Amit and Nisha flew to States for a fortnight. Ragini, as expected, did well in Pre-Boards despite the war scenario at home.

Over the next few days a new pattern of life style developed at home in which I was completely isolated. I was denied the opportunity to share their idle talk. I wondered what would change this stasis in our life. I planned to take a break, my boss refused to grant me leave.

I made another attempt at reconciliation in the night. I lightly touched Rati's arm and asked for forgiveness, she again rejected me. "You have shaken the very foundations of my life. Sometimes, I feel as if our relationship is lacking in legitimacy." She spoke with venom.

I could not sleep, and tossed till late in the night. I woke her up, and asked, "Do you want divorce?"

"Can't you discuss this at a more earthly hour? It is past two." She was composed, and in full control of the situation.

My teeth chattering with seething anger, I went to the store, took out the spare quilt, and shifted to the `divan' in the drawing room. I refused to go back to my wife even though the cold wind sneaking in through a crack in the windowpane made me shiver.

Her behaviour turned me paranoid, and after more than two decades I again relapsed into morbidity. I wept, breaking into hysterical sobs. But no one came to alleviate my pain.

Ours had been a happy family. Whenever in rough weather, we had gone to each other—held each other's hands, kissed away all the pain, and resentment—and made up. It seemed so simple.

Rati had given me immense happiness. She understood my needs, pains, and filled me with pride and love. Impulsive, Rati could get joys out of trivial little things, and carry me along with her. We could get ecstatic watching the sunrise from the bed of the ocean at Tondi, in the backwaters of Tamilnadu, or gazing at the resplendent full moon on a wintry night. Once while staying in a Guest House at Mussorie, she woke me in the dead of the night in late November. "Look, Arvi," she pointed out at the lights of Dehradun. The lights down below glittered like a long diamond necklace suspended in the air. The moonless sky above was studded with diamonds. "It is a world of diamonds," she whispered, "the diamonds of joy". We brought our chairs and a blanket. In the freezing cold, we huddled like children watching the glory of god. It was so majestic, and divinely beautiful that both of us had tears in our eyes. Often, we reminisced of that cold night, and were filled with warm, tender emotions. How could I forget those joys that we had shared in the past? And then together we had created Ragini — the sweetest child in this world. How could Rati behave in this way because of what happened so many years back?

Ragini, who learnt to say papa, and mama in my lap; crawl and walk with my help; whom I taught 'a, b, c,', played, and skipped around with me — her animus towards me jolted me. In any quarrel, she sympathized with her mother but made sure not to ignore me. She ran around between the two of us trying to diffuse the tension, saying and doing the right things so that harmony was maintained and both of us, at the first opportunity, could bury our differences. This time she was against me. The conflict was ballooning out of proportions and scourging our lives.

A month passed. Each day was a pain. I realised there was a rhythm in sorrow too as there was in daily routine. I decided about the various options in life so that Rati and I could separate. My mind worked hard, yet I was indecisive. Living a life without Rati was like spring without flowers. It was frightening that the avalanches sweeping across our lives, and threatening our relationship had their origin even before our marriage.

Winning over Ragini was crucial for me. I decided to buy her a pair of Levi jeans that she had been pestering for some time. After office, I drove to Connaught Place. While walking in the corridor, someone patted on my back. I turned to find Parminder smiling at me. We sat over a cup of coffee, talked over the past, and I blurted out the incident relating to his diamond watch, the havoc it had again caused in my life, and how my marriage was at the breaking point. He turned grave, and then suddenly broke into a smile.

"Forget it," he said. "Let us meet over dinner during the weekend."

I accepted the invitation.

Rati refused to join me, but when Parminder talked to her, she agreed.

Parminder lived in Chanakyapuri facing an embassy. At the entrance, he and his wife hugged us warmly. A sprawling lounge with heavy sofas, a long glass table in the dining room, an original of Amrita Shergill gilded in golden frame, and a gushing fountain in the vast lawn at the back reminded us that Parminder belonged to a different class. But Rati and I were unhappy to see Amit, and Satish already well ensconced with their spouses, and laughing merrily over something.

"We were talking only about you," said Satish, who was respectably attired in a suit and a tie today. "Somehow, Amit and I did not expect that you would have the cheek to turn up again."

Both of us wondered why Parminder had invited us to undergo another humiliation. Rati glowered at me, and refused to touch the snacks being served. Parminder walked over to Rati, ferreted out something from his inner coat pocket, and handed over to her.

"This is the famous diamond watch of my sister, which has again brought a crisis in Arvind and your life."

Everyone was stunned into silence.

"You can pass it around. But this time I am keeping a watch on it because we do know that one of us present here is a thief."

We all had a good look at the exquisitely designed antique watch studded with diamonds. When the watch was again in Parminder's hands, in walked a pretty girl who was introduced as Harjot, Parminder's niece.

Amit's face turned pale.

"About six months back, Amit had walked into our new showroom on Janpath and wanted to dispose it off," Parminder said. "One look at the watch and I recognised it. Harjot had struck the deal of more than a lakh and I, sitting in the back office, had approved it. Here is the photocopy of the receipt with Amit's signature." Parminder waved it. He looked angrily at Amit and added, "Now, will you admit to the stealing of this watch in college or do I call the police?"

Cornered, Amit confessed to the theft, and left with Nisha.

"Thanks for keeping your promise, and saving my marital life," Rati said to Parminder. He clarified that after getting the watch, he had wanted to contact me, but could not reach me. After the accidental meeting with me, he had arranged the get - together as he had Amit's mobile number from the receipt.

On the return journey, the whole world seemed to glitter like diamonds.

■ ■ ■

Broken Pieces

As I step out of the cool ambience of T&N Sons Jewellers, Lajpat Nagar with a red gilded box, I feel roasted by the blazing June sun. With the mercury soaring to 45 degree Celsius, it is hot as hell. Last month, we were blessed with a son; the necklace is a gift for my wife, Nidhi. She had spent hours at half a dozen shops before selecting it. The necklace needed the matching string, and here I am, soaked to the skin in perspiration.

I start the car and negotiate through the crowd when it suddenly breaks down. Fuming, and cursing, I locate a garage; the mechanic promises to have it repaired in an hour.

Unfamiliar with the market, I decide to search for a decent restaurant to escape the heat. While walking on the pavement, a hawker selling corn sticks blows the coal dust right into my face. I rush to a tuck shop, clean my face with water and order a cola. I notice a young couple with a four- or five- year- old son insisting on an ice cream but the father rejects his demand. The boy, in defiance, kicks at his father's shin, and arrogantly moves ahead. I wish I had a streak of insubordination in me.

Disobedience is alien to me; the trait of rebellion perhaps does not exist in my DNA. Though born under the powerful Leo sign, I have never taken any decision in life. Others decide for me. First, it was my father. My education, career, my friends, my hobbies, my marriage, court proceedings for divorce — everything was determined by him, till he died four years back without solemnizing my second marriage as predicted by the astrologers.

Immediately after my first marriage, Supriya took over this onerous responsibility for about five years. It was not that I had not tried to act like an adult, I had, but each time I blundered, Supriya had to go to a great length to retrieve the situation. It was much easier to leave everything to her. A graduate from Miranda House, she was sophisticated, cultured, well read and endowed with artistic propensities. I had never been to a college as I was forced by my father to join a Diploma course in engineering after school.

In fact my marriage with her had come as a surprise to me. The only daughter of an Executive Engineer in Central Water & Power Commission, she was excessively pampered by her five brothers. Unfortunately, a broken engagement ruined her prospects in the matrimonial market. When my father, an Assistant Engineer, approached Supriya's father for her marriage alliance with me, her father jumped at the offer, and marriage was solemnized within a month. Supriya gave me lot of happiness, and took complete control over all the facets of my life except the few hours I spent in the office.

I am an Executive Engineer in the Irrigation Department, and hope to be a Superintendent Engineer before I retire. At the office, I implicitly obey my bosses. Whenever I have to decide, I go by the judgement of my subordinates. I do not have the spine to take any decision on my own. Once alone, without any aide, I was forced to pass a certain order. My hands had turned damp and sticky and I felt a shooting pain in the pit of my stomach. When the attendant brought the afternoon cup of tea, I had told him all the particulars of the case, and asked, "Ramdin, Theek heh ne?" (Ramdin, is it OK?) The old man had nodded and I got the confidence to sign the file. But it was not easy.

My father had unilaterally decided on the divorce proceedings; I had no say in it. I wanted to take the custody of Esha, my daughter, but was overruled by my father, brother, and his wife. "She will be as rotten as her mother," was the unanimous opinion of all the relatives.

Without much protest, I signed the papers my father gave me and tendered evidence as advised by the advocates. Sometimes I did not approve of what my father was doing, I felt I was being unfair to Supriya, but the will to stand up to my father was lacking. For twenty two years, Supriya glowered and sniped at me in the court. She abused me openly, and screamed at me whenever we met. I did not hit back.

I have seen my daughter grow from a toddler to a beautiful girl, a replica of her mother, only in the court complex where she turned up rarely. When she was about seven or eight years, I had overheard Supriya telling Esha, "There goes your father who is responsible for ruining our lives." And she pointed a finger towards me. It had bruised me, but I was helpless. With years, Esha ignored me all together as if I did not exist. I had tried many times to attract her attention; she would not even glance towards me. Once, trying to avoid a porter carrying a heavy load, she had collided with me. She raised her eyes; the coldness in them bore into mine, as if ripping me apart. Her indifference was more piercing and hostile than her mother's hatred. And coming from one so young, and a part of me, I bled.

Immediately after my father's death, Supriya agreed to the divorce, and I gave her one of the two houses. I allowed my elder brother and his wife to manage my affairs, and was surprised to learn that their intentions were not above board.

Nidhi breezed into my life, and swept me off my feet. Before I landed on the ground, she had forced me into marriage. Perhaps on my own accord, I might have wavered but she gave me no time to reflect.

Nidhi is better organised than Supriya; she has the experience of two marriages and a son through each marriage. She inherited a taxi service from her father and his junior partner as well. Supriya was generous and large hearted whereas Nidhi is miserly, and settles for second hand stuff. Old taxis, old houses, old furniture, old garments, and second hand husbands. Sometimes I suspect that the newborn is not my son but of the elderly turbaned partner, who has been more loyal to her than her former husband. However, she looks after me, and mothers me to no end. She manages all my investments, and has relieved me of all responsibilities.

Overtly possessive, Nidhi does not allow anyone to share her personal belongings. Fortuitously, about three months back, I wore her sneakers, and she created quite a scene. "Dare you make such a mistake again?" She threatened. Shocked by her over-reaction, I wonder even now whether I have made a major mistake in marrying her. Maybe I am not lucky in marriage.

I keep on comparing Supriya and Nidhi; it comes naturally to me even though I do not want to. Maybe I am still fond of my first wife. It was Supriya's sharp tongue that ruined our lives. Being a feminist, she talked to men on equal terms, and was not unduly reserved in their presence. Unfortunately, my father came from a very orthodox background and disliked her uninhibited behaviour with men. He complained often about it, I persistently ignored him in the broader interest of harmony. The situation grew tense when my father, after retirement, settled down with us.

Once, at a party at our place, she laughed freely with her best friend's husband; it could be misconstrued as mildly flirtatious. My father could not take it, and chastised her, and she retaliated. One argument led to the other.

"You talk and behave like a loose woman," he shouted at her. "Shut up, you old fool!" She screamed back at him.

I was confused, my legs trembled, and I did not know what to do; I had always feared this confrontation between the two.

The old man never forgave her.

When Supriya went to her parents for a day, he hired a truck, and brought all the household goods of our house to my elder brother's place. Six months later, an application was filed for divorce proceedings.

What I have missed out most in life are the happy moments I had spent with Esha. I vividly remember how on my return from office, she would throw her arms around my legs, and hug me hard. When I hurled her in the air, her eyes sparkled with laughter, her brownish hair fluttered in the breeze and turned golden in the light of the setting sun. A gift from the gods, she brought happiness and sunlight in my life. That little Esha is lost somewhere in the bitching at the court complex, in the arguments of the lawyers, the snide comments, stares of the judges, the relatives, and the audience. The labyrinths of time have swallowed her, and turned her animus.

Failure as a father hurts me most. Sometime I wish I had a magic wand, and could turn the clock back, and be more supportive to my family! I look outside the shop, and to my pleasant surprise notice Supriya, and Esha talking animatedly, unmindful of the biting sun. Maybe I am daydreaming? I jerk myself, pay the shopkeeper, and race after them. When I am able to catch up with them, I am panting. "Supri," I raise my voice. She stops in her tracks, and turns.

"Oh Vinod!" She smiles, and looks elegantly pretty. I am relieved that she has no bitterness. "How have you been?"

Observing that Esha has continued walking, she catches up with her and reprimands her. Esha does not acknowledge my presence and refuses to walk back. I stroll over to them.

"If you have some spare time, let us sit somewhere." I suggest, my heart pounding wildly.

Supriya looks at her watch. "Why not? We have an hour or so. We can cool ourselves and escape this wretched heat."

My daughter protests; Supriya puts down her foot, and Esha, unwillingly, gives in. Supriya is familiar with the market, and guides us to a posh place on the first floor. "Thank God," she says, on our behalf, as she occupies a central table.

Esha has not glanced towards me even once; I can see a sparkle in her eyes, which is alien to her. Throwing her bag on a chair, she disappears in the washroom.

"How is Nidhi?" Supriya asks beckoning the waiter.

Making myself comfortable in the plush sofa, I feel relaxed. It is like old times.

"She is busy with the baby and her taxi service?"

"And how is her partner?"

I colour, and am hurt. Perhaps I made a mistake in inviting her.

"Sorry," she says. "I was being bitchy but it has become a habit."

I understand what she has gone through, and let it pass.

The thought that I had not discharged my responsibility of arranging a marriage alliance for my daughter had been gnawing at me for the last few years. Despite our differences, I had repeatedly asked Supriya to find a suitable boy for Esha. "How can she marry? She hates all men after seeing the behaviour of her father," was her usual reply.

The first time I heard it, I was rendered speechless; nevertheless, I have persisted assiduously.

"How is Esha?" I inquire, and realize I should not have asked; she is sure to hit back, and tell me to find out personally.

"She has decided to marry." Supriya smiles at me as if she has scored a point over me.

"I am so happy," I whisper. Tears hover around the corners of my eyes. "Thank you Supri, thank you."

Thrilled with gratitude, I grasp her hand. I have touched her after about three decades. Our hands quiver, the old chemistry is at work. I have never thought of any other woman till Nidhi forced me into marriage though I know from reliable sources that Supriya had many flings after the initiation of court proceedings. Chairman of school selection committee, the principal, the advocate, and so on.

"We could have been so happy if only you were more supportive—"

I nod, but it is useless to talk of it. It is in the past.

I turn and see my daughter gossiping with some friends.

Supriya tells me Esha is marrying her school colleague, and the marriage is fixed after about 20 days. She invites me to attend the ceremony, and talks endlessly of her prospective son-in-law and I listen like a responsible, concerned father, asking questions, going into details. She shows me the marriage card, and I appreciate its simplicity, and design.

The waiter brings the order. Sipping coffee, I resolve on something, and look at Supriya. "Can you do me a favour?"

I am bubbling with a new confidence, and she looks at me with surprise, and nods. I hand her the box containing the necklace. "I want to give this to Esha, I need your help."

She understands that Esha will not accept it directly from me. She takes the box and opens it.

"Fantastic! It is a work of art." She exclaims and marvels at the delicate work. And then she looks doubtfully at me. "Did you not buy it for Nidhi?"

"Yes, but I want to give it to my daughter." I am emphatic.

"Are you sure?" she asks again despite my confidence. Perhaps she suspects Nidhi will chew me up alive. She is right but I hold my ground and say, "Of course."

Esha returns to her seat, and looks at the sparkling gold necklace. She takes it from her mother, and is more euphoric in praise than her mother.

"It is exquisite." She smiles radiantly. "For whom is it?"

"It is for you, my darling." Supriya pats her daughter affectionately. "Your father has given it to you on your marriage. Accept it, my love."

"What?" She shrieks, and pushing the table rises. Some china pieces clatter, and crash down. She glowers hard at me; the dormant volcano becomes active, and erupts. Her face is contorted with seething anger.

"I don't know this man — who is he?" She screams at the top of her voice like a paranoid. With tears rolling down her cheeks, she picks her bag and runs out of the restaurant.

For an instance, a hush falls. Many heads turn towards us. I do not have the courage to raise my head and look at my ex-wife. Slowly, Supriya places the necklace carefully in the box, closes it, and hands it back to me. Her face has turned ashen, and she looks vaguely at the shards of china.

She gets up from her seat, and in the process adds to the breakage of the crockery. She whispers a goodbye, and leaves.

I continue to stare at the broken pieces.

■■■

Souvenir From Switzerland

Fatigued and queasy after the first ever right- hand drive from Calais, I turned the car to a parking lot at Lile, Belgium, for a brief stopover. Without anyone to help me in reading the GPS and navigating the car, I was frustrated, and fumbled at every turn with the fear of smashing my car into some other vehicle. All the time I cursed Siddharth, my old class fellow and buddy who had forsaken me for a new girlfriend he had met only a day before. Sid and I had planned the trip to Grindlewald, Switzerland, a year in advance — actually it was his idea, and I had simply acquiesced — and had flown all the way from Delhi to meet him in London. But he had backed out the night before departure. A young French girl had moved into an apartment just opposite him across the side road, and he had been infatuated by her beauty though he could not muster the courage to talk to her for last three months. Only yesterday, he had been able to converse with her for a few minutes. No doubt the girl was stunningly pretty as he kept on emphasizing, but come on you don't ditch your friend of over ten- year standing for a girl with whom you have hardly spoken for ten minutes. She was so snooty that she had refused a cup of coffee at no less a place than the Ritz. He had invited her to Grindlewald and she had frowned, however, she smiled at the thought of a weekend in Lake District at his expense. No commitment, no assurance — a stupid smile — and the bastard was so smitten that he cancelled the trip.

With a pique, I had left the room, and decided to go ahead. After all, I had flown all the way from India for this only. Perhaps, I had taken on more than I could handle. I felt nausea. A hot glass of strong coffee, and a chicken sandwich kicked away the fuzziness. When I drove past Brussels, my spirits revved as I got used to the right hand drive, and GPS.

For the night, I was booked at hotel Novotel, Luxembourg. The chic girl at the reception looked quizzically at me when she asked, "You alone," and I nodded, a little confused whether she had thrown any hint at me. Nothing happened. Frazzled, I hit the bed, and dozed off.

After a sumptuous breakfast in the morning, I took to the road again. Driving alone can be dull and torturous. Though Sid's car was smooth on the road, his choice of audio CDs gave me headache, and I switched off the stereo. I kept on telling myself repeatedly that I was on a holiday, and had no choice but to make the most of it. Though, it was not easy.

I felt a sigh of relief on crossing the border into Switzerland, and had my first halt at Berne. When I went to the washroom I had to pay a Euro. Seventy rupees! A sound economy, an annoyingly efficient government, and the way they fleece you for everything, even for relieving yourself. After nibbling the sandwich, I walked down the stairs with coffee in my hand, and collided with a young girl.

"Sorry, sorry," she said dodging the hot coffee splashes on her red coloured top. I apologized. The girl, who appeared to be from the Subcontinent, was beautiful.

She took me by surprise.

"By the way, would you be having some change?" she asked, and offered me a twenty Euro note.

Politely, I declined.

"Actually, I need a Euro coin for going to the washroom," she said a little embarrassed, and looked prettier.

Understanding her predicament, I offered her a coin. "But how will I return it to you?"

"It is all right," I said. If Sid could cancel a trip, and lose a couple of hundred francs, I could at least blow a Euro on a lovely girl.

She thanked me, and dashed upstairs where the washrooms were located.

Despite his weird behaviour, Sid's choice of apartment was excellent. It was a two- bedroom flat in a huge chalet from where I could have a clear view of the snow clad mountains, and green pastures on the slopes at hardly a distance of a few hundred yards. It overpowered me. Something, I had seen in the photographs or Yash Chopra movies only. I was so cut up with Sid that I didn't call to thank him. "To hell with him," I muttered, and looked forward to enjoying the privacy of the entire place at my disposal for a week.

The holiday meant a lot to me. It was the first major holiday of my life, one who was turning thirty in next six months. Money was hard to come by. With the responsibility of five younger siblings — my father died when I was still in my teens leaving me to face the music — personal entertainment was ruled out. My grandfather had given us our share in the property, and we all including our mother cramped inside a two - bedroom flat in Old Rajinder Nagar, where even stretching the arms was a luxury. When the third sibling pitched in with a lucrative job, I decided to have a real break.

I cooked breakfast for myself, and headed towards `First', a stone's throw from the chalet with a sling bag containing Haldiram snacks, and a bottle of water. As I walked down the main market, someone shouted at me, "Hey!"

I turned, and found the same girl I had met at Berne waving, and smiling at me. She was at her breakfast in a restaurant right on the pavement.

I walked over to her, and pulled a chair opposite her.

"Where to — so early?"

I explained my mission.

"I'll join you," she said abruptly. "Of course, if you don't mind."

"I would love it."

She paid, and rose. Suddenly, she stopped. "I hope you had your breakfast," she asked with concern.

I nodded, and she smiled.

Minutes on, when a racing car almost brushed past her from the opposite direction, I pulled her away from the road as it was the most natural thing to do. It moved her, and she thanked me. She was at Grindlewald for four nights only. Later, she confided that she had come with a friend who had met her fiancé there, and she had moved to his hotel as pre-planned.

At the ropeway station, the girl at the counter gave us an option to buy the ticket for 80 francs or all the ropeway tickets (including the cruise in the lake at Interlaken) for 225 francs. The offer was tempting. The girl did not hesitate in buying the 225 franc pass, and as I was there for longer period, I too opted for it. She paid for the passes, and I gave her the money. She returned me one Euro saying, "We should go American. Strictly, fifty-fifty."

I nodded, and pocketed the Euro. Later, I felt a little sheepish, and returned the money. She refused. Ignoring her, I took her purse, and slipped the coin inside it. My gesture was a little unusual, and the ease with which I had touched her hand gave me a sweet sensation I had seldom experienced in life. Her large black eyes rested on me for an instant trying to understand me. I was sure it was not about money.

In the trolley, I explained about Sid. Strangely, she seemed more understanding of his attitude than I had been. "These things can happen," she muttered. En route, the trolley stopped at Bort and Schreckfeld.

"We will walk down from `First' to Bort," she suggested, and I nodded allowing her to take control of the situation.

`First' gave us a panoramic view of the snow clad mountainous range with early May winds tearing into us. Hot coffee and potato chips helped in warming us.

As we loitered in the open clicking our cameras, a signage suggested a lake at fifty minutes walk.

"How about it?" I looked at her, and she willingly agreed. It took us more than an hour. The unruffled bluish green waters of the Lake Bachalpsee with towering Bernese Alps in the backdrop were breathtaking. The cold breeze made us shiver, and we hastily retraced our steps. We had our lunch in the restaurant at `First.'

"Should we not get introduced formally," she said with a smile. "I am Sunaina Anand."

"Shekhar Arora."

She offered her hand, and it lingered in my hands for an instant.

I told her about my parents, my father's death, my five siblings, and how I had taken my engineering degree from Pillani and MBA from IMT, Ghaziabad, and was helping my family.

"No marriage plans," she asked.

"Ma is searching for a girl. It could materialize any time." She smiled and wished me good luck.

I learnt that she had obtained a degree in Management from Delhi this year, and was planning to join her father's hotel business. They had two hotels in Paharganj, their prestigious hotel in Gurgaon had closed down last month, and they were trying to buy something in East Delhi.

She seemed tougher than me. After the tiring journey to the lake I was exhausted, she goaded me to take up the challenge of walking down to at least Shreckfeld. It was one of the most pleasant journeys I had ever taken in my life. When we sat down on a piece of rock admiring the cattle grazing on the slopes and the ringing of the bells hanging from their necks, she opened my sling bag, and unzipped the 'bhujiyya' packet. After resting for a while, she rose, and caught my arm going down the steep incline.

I developed a companionship with her that I had not known for the last six years with any of my colleagues or friends.

Back at Grendlewald, I didn't want to miss out on her company, and invited her for a cup of tea at my place. She liked the apartment, went up to the small balcony, and almost gave a small cry of joy. "What a wonderful view?" she said, stretching her arms.

We planned dinner at a small restaurant she had selected. The restaurant was overcrowded. The head butler gave us a seat that was not easily accessible, and he made an elderly couple get up, and we squeezed through. The bald man winked, and smiled at Sunaina, and said, "Young lady, now you are cornered, and cannot move for the next hour or so."

Intimidated by the arrogant smile of the old man, she retorted, "I can jump over your head, sir."

When the waiter distracted my attention by asking me something about India, I overheard the old woman mumble a few words to which there was a rejoinder from Sunaina, and everyone laughed. I too smiled at them.

Wit and humour I adore in others because I don't have it in me. Sunaina went up in my esteem with her repartee. We both talked and talked about ourselves as we felt comfortable in each other's company.

Sunaina was fond of taking too much of water even in the chilling cold. At a time, 2-3 glasses were normal; usually, she carried her own water bottle.

The old couple waved at us before leaving. The old woman returned, hugged Sunaina, and said, "You two make a wonderful couple."

I had read that clichéd dialogue in fiction many times, strangely, it affected me. I started thinking of her as my life companion. The 3-4 girls my mummy had shown me in recent past were no match against her, both in brains and beauty. I am averse to skinny girls, fortunately, Sunaina was slightly plump.

The whole night, I thought about her.

Next day, we drove down to Trummelbach falls where the water from 3 or 4 mountains collects, and thousands of tons of water gushes down the fall. The lift goes up to the fifth level, and the levels from 6th to 10th have to be covered by foot. The lift man was a young handsome Swiss in his early thirties, robust and cheerful.

"You see those rickety stairs," he said with a poker face pointing at some disarrayed shafts of old decayed wood, which hardly looked like a staircase. Half- heartedly, some women replied, "Yes, please."

"Look at them carefully, ladies and gentlemen because after the point where this lift stops, you will have to take this staircase."

"Oh, no!" Men and women gasped in disbelief. Shocked at the revelation, we all stared at one another wondering whether the staircase would be able to support our weight or crumble down.

In the meanwhile the lift reached its destination.

"Here we are," he said ebulliently opening the door, and pointing at the proper staircase.

"Didn't I pull off a fast one?" With a twinkle in his eyes, he laughed heartily. It was greeted with a sigh of relief.

When we moved up the steps, we saw the frightening spectacle of the rushing waters as it disappeared in the bottomless pit. With each level, it grew more slippery, damp and awesome. At the highest level, a mist had settled, and the waterfall was at its wildest; the ambience, quaint and eerie. Sunaina moved closer to me and almost embraced me. The few people present were scattered far and wide, and tentatively, I kissed her. She didn't object.

We walked down the stairs from fifth floor to the ground level. After the exhausting journey, she preferred to walk in the nearby jungles instead of trying out a new tourist place.

"Should we not have coffee at your place watching the snowy mountains?" She suggested after dinner.

I gave my assent, and grabbed her arm.

"It looks like home," she said on reaching the chalet, and prepared coffee.

We sat in the balcony looking at the snowy mountains in the moonlit night, and her head rolled over my shoulders. When I placed my arm around her, she offered her lips, and I kissed them greedily. I took her inside the bedroom, and we made love.

"It was heavenly," she said.

At two in the morning, she insisted to go back to her hotel, and I escorted her in freezing cold.

The visit to Jungfrau, one of the highest peaks of Europe, was the most memorable experience of my life. We spent over four hours going through the Ice Palace containing many ice statues including that of Sherlock Holmes, and later skied on the ice with Jungfrau, Monch and Eiger mountains looking down on us. The sedate white snow on the mountain tops and the slopes, the snowfield stretching downwards like a glacier, the hushed whispers of the tourists as if they were afraid to spoil the quietude of the abode of gods, the pleasant chill in the warm bright sunlight, and the entire snowscape: it seemed like a dream. Despite the nip in the air due to a gentle waft of breeze, romance was in the air. Or was it the effect of Sunaina? Overwhelmed by the magic of the Alps, I moved with my companion towards the mountains, a little farther from the tourists, and asked her, "Will you marry me, Sunaina?"

"Yes, my love."

Facing the Eiger and Monch mountains, we kissed each other lightly.

In the night when she lay in my arms, she felt at ease, and didn't insist on going back to her hotel.

At Mannlichen, we were trapped in the pouring rain while going up the highest point from where the view was exhilarating. On the return journey, we were enveloped by the clouds, and lost our way. The fear of slipping, and going down in the valley below haunted us through out, and surprisingly, it brought us closer. Later, in the restaurant, she asked me, "Are you serious about our marriage?"

"Yes, I am."

"But we hardly know each other."

"What more is there to know?" I said confiding a secret buried deep in my heart. "I knew a girl for almost seven years and she just left me one day and married an IFS (Indian Foreign Service) bloke whom she had met for the first time through her parents."

That settled it.

On the way to Murren, the same day in the afternoon, we were befuddled at the sight of the endless snowy range of mountains at such close quarters. When she saw a hotel called Alpine, she told me, "We will come here for our honeymoon."

That night she sent me into ecstasy with her love and passion. Wrapped only in a blanket, we sat in the balcony sipping coffee, and watching the moonlight glide on the snow-capped mountain. It seemed unreal, almost like a fantasy!

Though the morning was bleak and cloudy, we stuck to our schedule and went to Interlaken. The cruises in the lakes Brienzersee and Thunersee were extremely enjoyable.

In the afternoon, she suggested that we should repeat our visit to `First', and I endorsed it. The weather was perfect. Not a shred of cloud in the sky, and the pleasant sun travelling towards the western horizon smiled down on us. Seated in the open restaurant, we planned our lives. We decided to have the marriage in the first week of December, the date, location, the number of guests: everything was earmarked, and jotted down on a piece of paper. She expressed her thoughts on the kind of the house we would buy, and I agreed to her suggestion.

We spent 4-5 hours discussing almost everything, and she continued to sip water. It was almost evening. The restaurant was about to close, and we hurried up. The bill was over seventy francs, and I paid with the credit card but I couldn't control the scowl on my face. The waitress had charged twelve francs for six glasses of water Sunaina had consumed.

"Twelve francs for water!" I lost my cool. "Damn it. Eight hundred and forty rupees down the drain!"

"It's all right, Shekhar."

"What is all right, eh? You don't seem to care for money at all! I have five siblings and a mother to feed. How will we manage?"

Sunaina's face lost its colour.

"How much water can a person drink? Come on, how big is your tummy?" I said fuming with anger gesturing with my hands wide open. "Is it the size of a cow?"

At the back my mind I knew it was an inappropriate analogy, but those damned cows were everywhere in the landscape; I could see many of them down below.

I continued to scold her for overspending.

"All right," she answered. "You charge it to me."

"It is not a question of twelve francs but the principle involved. You have no respect for money."

Her patience gave way. "What nonsensical principle are you talking about?" She scoffed at me. "You are a bloody miser. Get out of my life."

Her hands trembling with rage — she took out 13, and not 12 coins — and hurled them on my face, and ran away towards the cable station leaving me alone in the restaurant to collect the coins. It hurt my face, and tore my heart apart.

My efforts to mollify her failed and she screamed at me when I tried to make amends at her hotel.

"For twelve francs you have insulted me as if I am a criminal," she shrieked. "Don't you dare to come here again otherwise I'll call the police."

She refused to take my calls in the night.

In the morning, when I knocked at her door, she had already checked out.

Switzerland lost its charm. The snow clad mountains, and swathes of green pastures with innumerable cows reminded me of Sunaina and I pined for her. Unable to stand it beyond a point, I went back to London next day. Boarding the first available flight to India, I returned home, a broken man.

I still have those thirteen coins as a souvenir; it reminds me of my stupidity.

■■■

Sea Change

On a late December afternoon, I stretch myself on a bench, and like the feel of the cool breeze sweeping across the Nehru Park. The park is my refuge whenever I quarrel with Megna, my wife. The myriad trees, the outstretched lawns solace me and help me maintain my equilibrium. I am going through a difficult period in life, though it is true that I never had it easy like my other school friends, and have envied them for their ready acceptance of things around them. They liked their job, did well in their lives and are happy. Those who did not like their profession initially have adjusted; their only ambition is to earn as much money as they can by any means. I am the only round hole in a square peg; I refused to accept my lot, and turned out to be a wet blanket for my family.

The sun is bright and warm but some stray white clouds are floating against a pale blue sky. I close my eyes and place the forearm on my forehead to ward off the sun glare. The past haunts me, and I relive my childhood as if it was yesterday.

Of the countless memories of my childhood, the most impressionable one is that of snuggling to my mother and holding on to her bikini strap to protect myself from the violent sea waves; I was so scared that I had shrieked wildly despite the boisterous laughter of my parents. The fear has been with me ever since, despite having spent more than twenty five years in the merchant navy. Unlike my forefathers, who were excited by the very sight of the sea, my stomach develops the cramps. I am told that my mother had met my father in the heart of the sea; I was conceived on a beach, and was born aboard a luxury cruiser somewhere in Europe. But I am mortified at the sight of the sea, and its roar sends a shiver down my spine even now when I am in my late forties. I have kept it a closely guarded secret from everyone except my parents.

It was my mother who noticed it; my father refused to believe it. Whenever he took me to the beach, he looked hard at me and was frustrated on seeing my terror- stricken face. Unable to accept such a reaction from his youngest son, his favourite, he increased the visits to the sea so that I would get over thalassophobia. I panicked at the sight of the sea, and tried to unclasp myself from my father's firm grasp. But he continued to drag me on the sand till we reached the waters and then flung me on the rushing waves. My body did not react. On being carried away by the receding waters, my father pulled me up again. Later, my father changed his strategy. He caught both my hands and feet in his powerful hands, threw me on his shoulders, waded through the waters and dropped me in the sea. Terror seized me. I cried and tried to run away towards the shore, he again pushed me into the waves. I kept on struggling against them till I fainted. With increasing visits, I stopped getting unconscious though there was no change in my attitude to the sea. The fear of sea remained and is as much a part of my life as having fish at meals. Whether it is the turquoise or emerald colours of sea or the rich white foam on the beach: nothing appeals to me. To me, the sea is a black monster chasing me for more than forty years and is out to swallow me, and is sure to succeed one day.

My father could not rationalize my reaction to the sea.

"You have cheated me." I overheard my father shouting at my mother. "He can't be my blood."

"You are insulting me!" She screamed at him. "A word more and I'll never see your face again."

It had shut up the old man. However, he was puzzled how his son could have such a fear psychosis when his last six generations had earned their livelihood at sea. A naval Captain in the Indian Navy, he was ashamed of introducing me to anyone. Not wanting to be rejected by the family, I turned out to be a good swimmer in the pool and won some awards also; it didn't change my father's opinion of me. I tried to win my father's approbation by having a swim in the sea with him. I was surprised that I didn't develop the cramps, and my father patted me on my back for the first time in my life. I repeated it several times, but even today I am paranoid of the sea.

I am a born idler; nothing holds my interest. I love to take a book and read in the cosy comfort of my bedroom especially if it is a cold rainy day. I prefer a novel or a novella; any other book is a pain. It was therefore not surprising that I didn't do well in studies. I like painting and sculpture; it didn't go well with my parents. My elder brothers had made it to the Indian Navy, Merchant Navy and Marine Engineering, and my father had chalked out my career also in one of these streams. But I had different plans. Unfortunately, my percentage in the boards was not good enough to enable me to get any respectable course in the university or to get into any engineering institute. I managed to join BSc (Pass Course) in Dyal Singh College. The next year I left this course, and shifted to History (Honours) at Hindu College. I didn't feel comfortable with it, and was toying with the idea of joining English (Honours) at St. Stephen's when my mother exploded. "Once your father retires he will not be able to help you and you will end up as a clerk somewhere." My father had been promoted as an Admiral some time back, and was due to retire shortly. The prospect of ending as a clerk in the docks pressed the panic button. I took the examination for Merchant Navy, and with my father's influence was able to join at TS Rajendra Institute, Mumbai formerly known as Dufferin College.

My years at Rajendra were uneventful and I was successfully able to hide my fear of the sea from my faculty members. I was aware that if it leaked out, I would be thrown out of the institute and even my father could not help me. The Director of the Institute, a close friend of my father, had a suspicion of it and stared at me. "Are you comfortable in the waters, son," he asked me point blank once. I smiled at him, nodded my head vigorously, and to prove him wrong dived from the highest point of the ship. Aware of my pedigree, he dismissed the thought with a shrug of his shoulder. I made extra efforts to show my enthusiasm and in the final year saved the life of a young recruit and bagged a medal also.

I met Megna, a hotel management graduate from Switzerland, in a party aboard the Vikrant and spotted her amongst 3-4 dozen glamorous girls. Maybe, it was the effect of the moonlit night, or the wine, I was infatuated by her. We dated for a month, and decided to get married.

The assignments on the sea were dull and cheerless. Nothing interested me on the ship: my colleagues' ribaldry or the rip-roaring laughter, the long bridge or rummy sessions and the interaction with my bosses, colleagues, and subordinates. But the endless asphalt sea was always there, ahead, behind and all around. There was no escaping it. I avoided looking at it and holed myself in my cabin at the first opportunity though it was not easy when on a ship. I worked in different companies to get over the monotony, the jobs ended wearing me down. Every trip to the sea sapped me of my energies, my zest of life though it made me richer, and my family happy.

Whenever at sea, I was thrilled on seeing the shore. The high-rise buildings, the shacks of the fishermen against the backdrop of the pale sky or the lighted buildings silhouetted against the dark sky excited me. My veins and arteries were recharged, and I could feel the blood flowing into them. The cities teeming with people, their smiles, laughter, frowns and tears, the women and children in colourful flowing dresses, moved me and sent a rhapsodic joy through me. Wading through bazaars humming with varied noises and din made me feel that life was worth living. I could hear the silence of the forests and the valleys and allowed myself to be buried in them for days together. When I looked at the snow clad mountains I felt god resided somewhere there. But the sea aroused no other emotion except that of fear.

With years, I rose in hierarchy and gradually was promoted as a captain. I was nonchalant about it though my wife was thrilled. The spells of rest on land increased, and I was happy to be with my wife and son. When my in-laws came over to stay permanently with us, I frequently escaped to other towns, and the mountains. My in- laws labelled me `irresponsible'; Megna let me have my way.

Sending shock waves in the household, I resigned. Unfortunately, the resignation was not accepted. The Chairman of the company knew my father and spoke to him. My father spent more than three hours with me.

"Sinha has told me that you have a big future in their company. You may end up on their Board of Directors."

This time I was firm and refused. But he persisted.

"All my life I have obeyed you — not now."

"Have you thought of the future of your son?" His tone was gruff.

I had always held him responsible for pushing me into the sea. "It is none of your business — it's my responsibility."

There was something in my demeanour and tone that hurt him grievously. He departed abruptly, and has not spoken to me since that day.

Megna tried to dissuade me from my decision; I was adamant.

"Maybe he needs a break," she told her parents apologetically. The break extended to three long years and still I could not decide whether I wanted to go back to the sea or not. A healthy middle-aged man not going to work and dependent on his wife is a social apostasy. Some felt I had misappropriated tons of money and was suspended by the shipping company, others held I was incompetent and would not be given any future assignment. My father- in- law's verdict was that I was lazy, a work shirker, and my mother-in-law stuck to her original opinion that I was crazy. She spoke with a lot of emphasis especially when my mother was around. My mother held Megna and her parents responsible for the sudden decision; in private, she told me that I was getting more obsessed of the sea than even my father or grandfather. Megna's ambition of sending our son to one of the best schools of England was shattered. Money was not a substantial problem for survival, yet some drastic adjustments had to be made in view of the dependence of my in- laws on me. With interest rates going down, their lifestyle underwent a radical change, and it discomfited them. I had suggested that we should shift from Anand Niketan to Gurgaon or Noida but was overruled.

I told everyone that I want to open a cargo company. No one

took me seriously and rightly because it was the remotest thought in my mind. I joined a painting school, and didn't make much progress. My sojourns to various parts of the country, and the company of my son kept me well occupied.

Two more years slipped by and I was still indecisive. The bickering increased and I started going to Nehru Park more frequently. Sometimes, I overheard my in- laws exchange heated words amongst themselves and use the word 'divorce' frequently. Fortunately, they speak in Kannada and I do not know the language; it does not upset me for the house is in my name.

Megna had come up with a number of options: going into business, trying for MBA, a job in merchant navy on the shore or a suitable assignment in the hotel industry. One of her colleagues, Pankaj Gupta, had opened an event management company and was keen to take me. I had vetoed all her suggestions. My ambivalence in not taking any concrete step in any direction distressed her.

I am ashamed to admit that I do not want to take up any job. Maybe, I have turned so lazy over the last five years that I find myself incapable of doing justice to any type of work. There is a lurking fear that if I take up anything, I am sure to goof it. I am scared of my incompetence, am afraid of failures and avoid taking any risks. The fear that I will be exposed has become an obsession with me. But I keep this as a secret, deep in the abyss of my heart, even deeper than the sea phobia. I guard it all the time and am scared that Megna should not get a whiff of it.

Once, Megna who has risen to be Deputy General Manager at the Taj Mansingh reminded me that it was too early to turn into a vegetable. Not getting any response from me she added, "There are more than three score canvasses in the basement — why don't you hold an exhibition?" She was quite optimistic that I would get some recognition and also make some money.

This was a new angle; I was not prepared for it. "I lack in professionalism." I blurted.

"Then be a professional." She retorted.

I engaged a private tutor; he was too snooty and we quarrelled within a week. I tried another tutor for six months, and then gave up.

"I paint for pleasure and not for money."

"Another Van Gogh!" she said bitterly. "You have not earned a dime for many years; it is hurting the family, Manav."

I offered to sell the BMW.

"Are you planning now to go in buses? A captain of the ship!"
"I don't mind. I am no longer a captain but an unemployed."

"What are you?" She jeered at me. "A painter who has lost his soul somewhere on the high seas or a painter searching for truth? Damn it, tell me."

Humiliated, I left the room.

I do not blame Megna for ridiculing me. In fact, I was amazed at the ease with which she had accepted the news of my resignation in her stride, as if an order for a wedding reception had been suddenly cancelled on the same day. She is basically a cool, gutsy woman and is always ready with a contingency plan. Perhaps, she is being rattled by her parents or maybe she is facing some pressures at the work place and refuses to confide in me. Gradually, over the last one year I have lost her love and respect, and it is manifested in her actions. Often, she stares hard at me as if I am a criminal and misses no opportunity to snipe at me. All the nights are cold and I am famished of a woman's touch. Whenever I want to hold her hand, she jerks it. Has she decided to divorce me? I am not sure but something is cooking between her and her parents. I avoid my friends, relatives and have become a loner. I dream my ship has struck against the rocks in the tropic seas; I am the only one on the deck and the ship is sinking in the fathomless waters.

There is some merit in her remark that I am searching for my identity. In all my sojourns, my interactions with human beings, I have been trying to find the purpose of my living. Unfortunately, I am still going around in circles and have not been able to get out of the vicious cycle. By getting away from the sea, I felt, I had made a beginning but am still groping for a direction.

An empty plastic bottle hits me disarraying my thoughts and I hear a girl screaming from the other side of the hedge at someone. Ruffled by the missile, I rise with the plastic bottle in my hand, and walk over to the other side towards the girl. Her face flushed with anger, she continues to shout at a young man reclined against the trunk of a tree, sipping a coke placidly. She does not notice me; neither does the young man. The girl is dusky, sharp featured, pretty and has an air of youthful arrogance. The young man is fair, chubby cheeked with a little paunch; a mischievous smile continues to play on his lips despite the volatile eruptions from the girl. I am not amused by the total indifference of the couple to me for I realize I am looking rather foolish trying to make them acknowledge my presence.

"Will you two listen to me?" I suddenly raise my commanding voice, give them a piece of my mind and throw the bottle in the hedge.

An uncanny quietness descends. The pretty damsel is rooted to the ground and the young man looks dazed to see an intruder appear inopportunely amidst them. His smile disappears; he rises with alacrity, moves towards me and apologizes. The girl turns red with embarrassment, and regrets her misbehaviour, shaking her head vigorously all the time.

"We were having an argument." The young man explains.

"It is O.K." I turn magnanimous and laugh a little. "I am also used to such demonstrations from my wife."

I cannot rationalize why I quoted Megna. She has never done such a stupid thing in her life; she is too level headed for such tempestuous exhibitionism in a public place.

I like the couple, especially the girl. Somehow, she reminds me of Megna during our courting days. I want to talk to them, and hang around for awhile. Appreciating that I am poaching on their privacy I slip away after wishing them well in life.

A week later, Megna hands over a letter to me in the evening. It is an offer by a newly established shipping company to captain their ship for a year. The terms of the contract are reasonable though not attractive—certainly not good enough for a naval officer of my credentials. Six years back when I resigned, I would get such letters frequently; this one has come after almost a year. I sense the hand of my father or elder brother in merchant navy. I barely finish going through the contents when Megna looks up expectantly and I shake my head. Her face turns ashen. The expression of pronounced hurt in her eyes touches me and before I can say something, she disappears in the washroom and bangs the door shut.

Over dinner, she stares at me repeatedly. At times, she is angry and on other moments sullen. I am aware she wants me to explain why I have refused the contract. She is perhaps worried that I may not get such an offer in future and it is likely she is right, she is seldom wrong in such matters. I do not want to indulge in any explanation in presence of my in - laws and am waiting for them to leave the table. Aware of the contract, they want to know my reaction and yet are reluctant to ask. They take all the time, even a second helping of the dessert. Convinced that I will not open my mouth in their presence, they give up and retire to their room.

Megna is edgy at my over reticence, leaves the table, and buries herself in the lounge sofa. I am the last to leave the dining table. Slowly, I walk over to her, touch her bare arms, and she snaps back with a jerk. Suddenly, it flashes across me that this is her contingency plan under operation. I take a seat opposite her and slowly, choosing every word carefully tell her that the terms of the contract are rather humiliating, and more important, I am mentally not prepared yet. Aware of her forthcoming reaction I hastily add, "You are aware that I don't like the job."

She flares up reminding me that she also did not like the night shifts ten years back but suffered it for the sake of the family. "I did not kick up the job," she adds vehemently.

I am defenceless.

"You are absolutely right, Megna, but I am not ready yet. Bear with me for some time more. Maybe something will turn up, which I would love to do."

Megna indulges in a long rhetoric on compulsions of human beings and how we must bow down before insurmountable circumstances and when they are favourable, grab the opportunity and try to achieve our ambitions. For an instant, she stops, turns her head and looks directly towards me. "Are you, by any chance, lacking in self confidence?"

Fortuitously, I am sitting in the corner of the sofa where the shadow of the pillar protects me and she cannot see my pale face clearly. I collect myself, and force a smile. "You can draw any conclusion you want to, Megna. I am in no position to defend myself."

I rise and shut the door of the study. It was close, very close. The fear of being exposed haunts me the whole night.

Pulling the rug under my feet, Megna announces one evening after dinner that she is putting up an exhibition of my paintings after four months at Treveni Kala Sangam. She had completed all the formalities.

"How — how could you do this to me, Megna?" My voice quivers a little as I look at her. "You are going to make a fool of me."

"No, I am not," she says confidently. "My gut feeling is that god has destined that you should be a famous painter."

She has taken on the mantle to accomplish what she feels is ordained by god. My pleadings have no effect on her.

For a week, I hole myself in my room on the attic. It is here that I fool around with my brush. In protest, I do not touch the brush.

A knock during a weekday upsets me from sleep. I open the door and find my wife smiling at me.

"Would you help in the selection and mounting of canvasses or I do it myself?"

Her eyes assess me intently, wander all over the room and again rest on my face. Megna has the habit of forcing her will on others ruthlessly. Behind the façade of the smile, I am aware there is no escaping her resolve.

"The exhibition is on." I smile back, and she breathes a sigh of relief.

For the next three months, I pour myself over the paintings, touching them up, redoing some of them with Megna hovering around me throwing hints. When I do not respond, she frowns. She has me all prepared for the opening of the exhibition at Treveni art gallery in late April by Minister of State for Tourism. Megna is able to muster about fifty guests and 2-3 journalists; the Minister is unable to make it.

After the function, no one even peeps in the Treveni gallery whereas three other exhibitions at Shridharni, Art Heritage in the basement, and the room adjacent have many visitors. Somehow it disturbs Megna more than me. I can feel that she is getting desperate. A young couple strays in after seeing other exhibitions and is about to leave when Megna blocks them and cajoles them to appreciate the canvass of an old man lost in his loneliness. "It is good, very good," the girl mutters, and hustles her hubby out of the room. Her face wrought in frustration, Megna collapses on the chair beside me.

"It's OK, Megna." I touch her lightly on the shoulder, which she does not appreciate and instead looks spitefully at me holding me responsible for the unfortunate episode. Suddenly, she rises from her chair. "I've to go to the office." She walks up to the door, returns, slightly touches me on the arm, and leaves abruptly.

The room is quiet again, almost like my attic. I pull another chair and rest my legs on it. I have chosen a corner with my back towards the door. I close my eyes and am lost in my vague thoughts.

The noise of the shuffling steps disturbs me. I do not turn my head expecting that the person will complete the round and walk away. When I do not hear the sound of retracing steps I slowly get up and walk towards the visitor rubbing my eyes.

"Oh, hello!" The Nehru park girl is smiling at me. She looks more carefree than the last time I saw her, and more pretty.

"Are these your paintings?"

I nod.

"Somehow, I had the feeling that the exhibition was put up by a very pretty woman." She grins broadly at me.

"My wife." I reciprocate her smile.

She turns her head towards the paintings and speaks casually as if giving an expert opinion, "Two- three of them are good," she says and points towards the canvass of the old man and the second one of a child playing with her mother. "But this is the best."

It was the painting of a couple sitting on the bank of a river, the woman's head resting on her man. I had titled it `the couple'

"There is so much tenderness in this scene" she says her eyes glued to the canvass "as if they are satisfied, contented after love-making and confident of each others' love. Such expression is not easy to capture."

She shifts her eyes towards me.

"But I do not approve of the river—it has spoiled its depth and beauty. If I were you, I would put the sea instead of this river."

"I do not like the sea." I blurt out spontaneously.

For an instant, she is perplexed and then catching my sleeve says, "Come, I'll explain what I mean."

She takes me to the adjacent room where another exhibition is on. "Look at this painting," she says pointing to a large sized canvass.

My eyes survey the room. Most of the canvasses have sea in it. The canvass where she has stopped has the same theme as my painting.

"My painting is nothing compared to yours — I have not been successfully able to give expression to the intimacy and tenderness between the couple but I have used the sea colours to express the same. If you were to introduce the sea instead of the lousy drain, yours would be a masterpiece."

Quietly, I see her paintings.

"Congratulations. You are a much better artist than me." I compliment her. "And you are obsessed by the sea."

She nods and adds, "I was born in Chennai and have spent major portion of my childhood in the south. My father is a photographer with Express."

I go back to the painting we were discussing earlier. "Don't you think the sea would dwarf the sensitivity?"

"No, if you are careful with the colours," she answers authoritatively. "If you need my help, I'm available."

"Thanks," I said wondering at the overconfidence of the young girl. Perhaps, my expression was too transparent, and she added with an impish smile flickering on her lips, "Come on, I am not a kid—I am married for three years. And you have met my husband."

"Oh!" I exclaim. I remembered the fair young man with a slight paunch. "I'll give a thought to your suggestion. Bye."

The whole night I work on the painting. I have never painted the sea before and run into a mental block for 2-3 hours when I try to convert the river into sea. I am convinced that the girl is right, still, it is not easy painting the sea. It does not come out the way I want, and I struggle with it throughout the night.

"You have spoiled it," Megna tells me when she sees it in the morning before going for her morning walk. Like a mother encouraging her off- spring that had repeatedly flunked earlier and has now passed with a compartment, she adds, "But thank God, I see a spark in you, which I have not noticed for the last many years."

She pats me lightly and closes the door.

"This will not do." Ritika remarks when she sees the modified canvass. "You are a novice at painting the sea." She brings her painting gear, pulls a chair and diligently teaches me how to paint the sea.

Later, sipping coffee on the steps of the open theatre of Treveni during lunch, Ritika talks of her cousin who is 12-13 years senior to her and is a captain in the Indian navy. "I am very fond of him. He is not only a dear cousin but also a friend. He loves the sea."

She loves to talk about this cousin whom she hero- worships. I nod, encouraging her to continue. I like her company and am mesmerized by the waterfall of her words.

"He says one has a lot to learn from the sea — its tranquillity, fury and depth. He is an amazing personality. Maybe, some of the sea has rubbed on to him."

She takes another sip, and tells me how she was introduced to the sea by her cousin, and her fascination for the sea.

"There is something of my cousin in you." She looks indulgently at me.

In one gulp, she finishes the cup and turns her face towards me.

"But why do you dislike the sea so much?"

I avoid her question with a smile. A friend of her spots her and walks over to congratulate on her exhibition.

I spend the next night also in the attic grappling with the sea colours.

"This is much better now." Ritika looks pleased, and personally hangs it on the wall adding, "But it can be improved."

Some school children visit Treveni and they are also chaperoned into my room. Half an hour later, an artist looks at the `the couple', nods his head appreciatively and moves ahead. Just before the closing of the exhibition, a middle-aged couple walks in leisurely and spends sometime looking around. "Not bad," the woman mutters and then resting her eyes on `the couple' whispers to her husband, "This is good," and the husband endorses it with a pat on her waist.

The visitor's book is blank but I am filled with little ripples of joy.

Ritika wishes me well, hands me a visiting a card and informs that some of the upcoming artists meet every Monday, Wednesday and Friday from 6 to 8 pm at the address given in the card. "I will be delighted if you could join us."

I thank her for the offer.

Later, I remember a night at sea when I could not sleep in my cabin and had climbed to the deck. It was the early hour of the dawn and the Pacific Ocean was calm and serene. I had a stroll and gone back to the cabin. Now when I recall that particular scene I realize it was magnificent.

Megna vainly looks at the papers for a review of my exhibition, and shakes her head with a look of disappointment. Ritika's exhibition has been well reviewed by two leading dailies.

I join the group and learn a lot from the budding artists. Ritika is patient and initially gives most of her time to me. In the next few weeks I paint many canvasses, most of them have sea. Megna is amazed at my synergy and feels happy that her idea of the exhibition had brought results. Ritika has a word of praise for my paintings. "You can capture the various moods of the sea even better than me."

A few days later, Megna informs me she has to go to Mumbai on an official visit. I talk to the Director of the Shipping Company who had offered me the assignment many months back. He is still willing to take me and throws an invitation to visit him for discussions on the grey areas.

"I'll be accompanying you to Mumbai to negotiate for better terms with the Director," I tell my wife. Her face lights up with an usual glow I have not noticed for the last few years.

"I'll take up the sea assignment. If it does not work out, I'll join Gupta's event management company. "

I place my arms around her shoulders. She looks up quizzically at me and without a comment hugs me.

■■■

Verdict

"Udey Shankar Murdabad! Down with Udey Shankar!"

The voices resounded in the air and rose above the din of the moving traffic on Shahjehan Road, Delhi. Udey Shankar, Supreme Court judge, looked at the people shouting themselves hoarse and smiled smugly. A dozen armed policemen were at the gate. Two days back, there had been an unruly mob of about six dozen men, now there were hardly half a dozen. All of them were demonstrating against his landmark judgement the week previous, directing the Delhi Government to shift all the polluting industrial units from the heart of the capital.

The masses had lauded the judgement because Delhi was heading towards becoming one of the most polluted cities in the world but the effected parties termed it highhandedness. Earlier, his judgment on clearing the illegal encroachments from the Delhi ridge area had upset the government.

Udey was pleased with the media reports describing him as an activist judge who had shaken up a sleepy, nincompoop government incapable of decisive action. He had taken upon himself the mantel of spearheading the environmentalists' crusade to protect the country from pollution. While attending social functions or appearing on TV, Udey was in the habit of passing value judgements on a large spectrum of issues, ranging from dowry deaths to India's relations with USA. With a handsome face, and a well built body, he had a charisma few could match. Judges were supposed to be reticent; his unconventionality disturbed his colleagues. Udey nurtured a secret desire to enter politics, and hoped to capitalise on his popularity at an opportune time.

His smile turned into a frown when he spotted Ramdin entering the bungalow in his dirty attire. The repugnant sight of the thin, gawky servant was sufficient to disconcert him. Ramdin handed over two packets of Dunhill in a tray to his master. Udey was about to thank him for bringing the reserve stock of cigarettes in the scorching heat of May when he noticed a drop of sweat slide from Ramdin's hand and fall onto the tray.

"Why can't you wipe your bloody hand before you show your wretched face to me," he shouted.

"Sorry, Sahibji, I was already delayed and rushed straight thinking you may need it."

"You are always ready with an excuse. Get out."

Udey was known to be a suave, decent gentleman, one who had empathy for the lower strata of the society. His conduct, his decisions proclaimed as much. But Ramdin could rattle him even when he was at his best.

His father had thrust Ramdin on him. Thirty years ago, he had brought Ramdin from Allahabad and entrusted the boy, in his early teens, to Udey's care. "I owe a lot to his father. Now, he is your responsibility. Treat him like your brother."

Ramdin had been with him since then, and was always treated like a servant.

Udey and Ramdin belonged to the same village of Sukhiya, 20 miles from Allahabad, and were distant cousins. The thought that a couple of decades back he and his servant had the same progeny perturbed Udey. Ramdin took pride in talking of his relationship and Udey was ashamed of it. He stood for democratic equality and liberalism; the presence of the uncouth Ramdin in his house was an anachronism of nature and he held his father responsible for it.

From day one, when Ramdin had touched his feet and said, "Now you are my mai baap (my lord and master)," he emanated obnoxious smells like stray cattle. Ramdin had not changed much in last three decades, however, Udey had got used to his odours.

The judge believed that nature had created everyone for a specific purpose; his faith was jolted whenever he saw Ramdin. There was absolutely nothing good about the man. He made a mess of anything and everything — whether it was the kitchen, tending the garden, taking care of the pet, sweeping the floor or cleaning the car. He was a failure, a zero. Udey wondered at the purpose of his existence? Given to announcing verdicts, Udey had pronounced him worthless, a burden on society, and a parasite. At least, a dozen times he had considered throwing him out of the house, but remembered the promise he had given his father, and continued to suffer him.

Ironically, Udey never doubted Ramdin's loyalty, though he was in the habit of telling small lies, stealing cigarettes, and stray coins.

For the last many years, Ramdin had been attending to all the personal work of the master of the house. Initially, Udey panicked when entrusting any errand to him, now he accepted the associated blunders. He was aware that despite Ramdin's best intentions, he was incapable of handling any situation because of his rural background. Now, Udey had grown familiar with him, and had abandoned the thought of a replacement. "At least, he is better than these pushy Punjabis." He consoled himself.

Bullying Ramdin was a part of Udey's daily ritual; thereafter he was at peace with himself and the world around. It worked as a catharsis, a safety valve. Fortunately, the other family members were not as hostile to Ramdin.

The following Sunday morning, the protesters disappeared, though the placards denouncing Udey Shankar had not been removed. The number of policemen had also dwindled to three or four. Assuming everything was under control, the other family members went out leaving Udey and Ramdin at home.

Just before lunch there was a commotion outside. Ramdin rushed in to inform Udey that there were more than a hundred ruffians outside. Before he could go up to the balcony to crosscheck, some of the goons rushed in with sticks, and started smashing the furniture, and the crockery. Ramdin pushed Udey towards the stairs leading to the first floor. "Please lock yourself in a room and don't worry Sahibji, I'll take care of the bastards."

And then he thundered at the hoodlums, and told them to get out. They laughed at the bony man. Udey dashed upwards, locked himself in the toilet and called the police on the mobile.

Ramdin fought valiantly, was eventually overpowered and beaten to a pulp. The hooligans ransacked the house, and destroyed everything. Some of them were planning to set the house on fire, others had just pulled down the door of the toilet in which Udey was hiding, when two dozen policemen with Sten guns arrived, and fired in the air. Hearing the gunshots, the rabble dispersed.

Udey was rescued before anyone could harm him. He looked frightened; his legs and hands trembled as if he had seen the ghost of death. For quite some time he was numb, his lips refused to open, and he wore a vacant look. An inspector of police, saluted him, and assured that everything was under control. After taking a glass of water, Udey felt composed, and realized he had acute pain in his left arm. He had collided against the wall when he had rushed upstairs.

Udey was strong-minded, and could stand any mental pressure and agony but he was scared of physical pain. A little scratch could make him throw tantrums. And today it was just unbearable, and he created quite a scene. Fortunately, someone had phoned for an ambulance with a doctor.

Ramdin was sitting quietly in a pool of blood when the doctor arrived. He was a tall, arrogant Haryanvi Jat with a prominent scowl on his face. He spent a lot of time with Ramdin and then examined Udey. The judge was cut up with the doctor for having wrong priorities; he should have attended to him first.

"Put the man outside in the ambulance," the doctor ordered the nurse and applied an ointment on Udey's arm.

"Are you not taking me to the hospital?" Udey looked disappointingly at the doctor.

The doctor shook his head, and replied, "You are perfectly OK."

Wincing with pain, and hurt by the doctor's attitude, Udey lost his cool. "Don't you know that I am Justice Udey Shankar, and the other man is my servant?"

The doctor retorted angrily, "Judge Sahib, yours is a mere scratch, I've bandaged it as you are overreacting. Look at your servant! He is bleeding profusely and may lose his left eye, but he has not complained even once. At the risk of his own life, he has protected you. He is only worried about you, and you are thinking only of yourself!"

Two men carried Ramdin away on a stretcher. Open mouthed, Justice Udey Shankar stared at the doctor, and his team.

■ ■ ■

Uncertainty

Ambika rose from the easy chair and pushed the curtain slightly on one side. The Maruti Swift and her son's Honda City were parked in the driveway, the third car she had been expecting for the last two hours had not arrived. Except for the lashing of the gusty wind, there was no activity at the gate. Darkness had descended; the black grey clouds gathering in the sky looked ominous. The dark bushes and trees silhouetted against the dim garden light shook vigorously in the wind and appeared ghastly. "A storm is brewing, it's sure to rain in the night," she muttered, though the morning had been warm and pleasant. She was waiting for Siddharth, her ex-husband who was being escorted by their daughter Vidya from Chandigarh. Ambika was aware that Siddharth disliked the rain in winter, and it perturbed her. She switched on the pedestal lamp; its pale light added to the sombreness of the spacious lounge.

Lata, Siddharth's second wife, and Ambika's cousin had died of cancer about a year back. Siddharth was returning to Ambika's home after more than a quarter century. She could hear the movement of Aditya, her son in the adjacent room; the frequent calls from his wife discomposed him. When tense, he walked from one end of the room to other exactly like his father.

The decision to send Vidya was taken by the siblings; they had not consulted her. Vidya was the one who argued and quarrelled with her father for being unfair to her mother, and she was the one who was more effusive in her emotions. She wanted her parents to make up before she married, and moved to US.

With the younger one gone from the roost, and the elder one spreading her wings to fly, Ambika had little choice. She had another year as the principal of Hindu College, Delhi University but thereafter it was a long, lonely road ahead that she had to trudge all by herself.

Ambika, Siddharth, were class fellows for five years in Honours and MA at the Hindu College. She was the topper throughout, and he barely scraped through borrowing her notes. She loved economics, and he hated it. Just because he wanted to be with her, he had pursued the post graduation. Siddharth was tall, fair, and had the build of a wrestler; she was slender, and petite. His mother had been disappointed to see the prospective olive complexioned daughter-in-law.

"How can you marry such a dark girl?" she asked. "It is Ambika or no one."

The parents caved- in as they were afraid the couple would elope and marry.

Ambika got lectureship, Siddharth joined the State Bank of India as Probationary Officer, and they got married. He was always there by her side: changing nappies, warming the milk, tucking the babies in the bed and sometimes making love on the same bed. Together, they had great time except when she was moody and petulant. He was thoughtful, caring and retained a smile on his lips even when she screamed at him. Despite the pandemonium in the house, they were always in tune with each other. With two babies, a doting husband, her teaching and research doing well, she was on the top of the world during those five years.

When an innocent junior accountant in the bank was made a scapegoat in a major scam, Siddharth had stood by him, and invited the wrath of the officer fraternity. One day, he was shunted far off to Madurai in Tamil Nadu.

All hell broke loose. Ambika could not cope with the pressure and went to pieces. Her parents pitched in, yet it was not enough. Whenever he visited Delhi, she rebuked him for defending the junior accountant. "What do you think you are? A hero? Because of you, our lives have been ruined." It took her many months to get over the rancour.

Loneliness hit him hard, he felt miserable. He tried a posting at a place close to Delhi, his request was rejected. The next time he went to Delhi, he asked his wife, "Amb, let us be together. Resign and be with me."

Ambika loved him, it didn't really matter much to her whether he resigned or she put in the papers. The opposition had come from her parents. "Why should you think of resigning? You are brilliant and have a much better career than your husband."

She ignored her parents, and mentally prepared herself for shifting to Madurai. Braving a distance of over 30 hours of train journey with two small babies, she visited him during summer vacation, and met the principals of local colleges. They were non-committal, and advised her not to throw away her job. The husband and wife considered their financial position, discussed and debated for hours. Finally, she concluded that it was not a viable proposition to give up the job, and decided to maintain the status quo.

At night, she asked him, "If ever I move to Madurai — bag and baggage — what is the guarantee that you will not be transferred to

Gujarat or any other state?"

"No guarantee," he answered gravely. "But what do I do during the late evenings without you?"

She threw a small pillow at him, and laughed. "Find out a girl on makeshift basis there is no dearth of shapely girls here."

"Really?"

She switched off the light, and he buried her in passionate kisses.

It was at a conference at Chennai that he ran into Lata who was there with her friends on a holiday. She recognized him, and was quite surprised to learn that Ambika didn't stay with him. "It is very stupid of her," she said. She was younger, taller, and fairer compared to Ambika. She spent all the evenings with him, and he liked chatting with her. She had completed B Ed and was expecting a job at Indore. "If ever you get posted in M.P (Madhya Pradesh), I'll come over to see you."

Fortuitously, he was transferred to Bhopal after six months, and she made it a point to spend a weekend with him.

Sparks flew, their passion made them lose their head. When he went to Delhi, he disclosed everything to his wife, and apologized.

"F*, F**, F*** it is all you men want out of a woman," she shrieked.

Siddharth begged her to resign, and join him. "Why don't you?" She challenged him.

He refused. The thought of being dependent on her all his life was too much of a risk. He had already contemplated on the subject, consulted his friends, parents, and decided against it. She was too capricious.

"Break the relationship with Lata or I'll file for divorce." She threatened.

But it was not possible to stop a woman like Lata. A crazy lover, she was there every weekend to warm his bed and share his loneliness covering a distance of about 200 Kilometres. Every time she assured him and herself that it was the last time she would see him, nonetheless, there she was every Friday night; and he waited for her at the bus stop late in the night, the food, and bed ready for her. It was sheer madness but a madness he adored. The thought of her transformed him, and when he saw her from a distance in the bus he ran up to her. His hands were invariably on her back, and he wanted to hug, and kiss her.

He realized he was making a fool of himself. To get away from her, he shifted to farther south, at Thiruvananthpuram in Kerala. Shocking him, she left Indore, and took up a job in the local primary school. A couple of months later, they gave up the pretence of being friends. She moved into his house, and enjoyed all the perks of a wife. Initially, eyebrows were raised when he took her to social functions, gradually, she was accepted.

Ambika understood his dilemma. The youngest child in a family of seven siblings, he was lost in the numbers. No one cared for him. Devoid of the affection and attention of his parents, he searched for love outside the home. If he hit off well with some people and liked them intensely, he wanted to hold on to them. The emotional void was reflected in his demeanour and was transparent even to a stranger. His hunger for love reminded her of a street dog that had followed her for a long time on a wintry night more for warmth and attention than food. Solitude made Siddharth uncomfortable, and suffocated him. He had no reserves of emotional security to fall back on at Madurai or Bhopal. She could imagine him walking on the lonely roads of Madurai or Bhopal at night and return home only when he was dead tired. Handling his over sexual drive would not have been easy. At the first opportunity, he had surrendered himself into Lata's arms.

But it was not her fault that he was not at Delhi. How could she kick away her job and be with him? She had obtained Ph D, and was likely to get an offer of Readership in Delhi School of Economics, and her name was well known in research circles.

When she heard about Siddharth and Lata's live- in relationship, she fumed and fretted. Moral support was forthcoming from all quarters, even the most unexpected. Her in- laws had threatened their son to sever ties with Lata. The mother-in-law had visited Ambika, and sympathized with her. "How could he behave with you in this way? God will punish them."

"I'm planning to divorce him." She had suggested.

"Don't. Why make it easy for them?"

Ambika considered it: the old lady had a point. If she was not planning her second marriage, why allow them the satisfaction of an easy marriage?

He was in Delhi for an official meeting, and wanted to meet her, and the children. "You are not allowed to see the children, you are a bad influence on them." She said on the phone. Then, he invited her for lunch or dinner.

After pondering over it, she had agreed to meet him at 'Host' for lunch. Was it curiosity, or assertion of her right to meet her husband or an attempt to retrieve her lover? She was not sure.

She had dressed meticulously in a plain blue chiffon sari that he liked. A light make up with generous spray of the perfume that turned him on. But he was not happy to see her. She had grown thinner; her face was haggard with responsibilities of running the house, and lack of love. It made him sad, and he held himself responsible for her present state. In contrast, Siddhartha looked handsome: new love had suited him.

Awkwardly, he rose, and spilled the water glass. "Sorry," he muttered, and beckoned the waiter.

She looked minutely at him, and asked sarcastically, "After three long years, why this honour?"

"I have come to ask for a favour. I want divorce."

"Not granted," she said abruptly, her eyes turned liquid.

He felt he had made a mistake in raising such a delicate issue in a restaurant. She might create a scene, and he might not be able to handle the situation.

"How is Vidya? And Aditya?"

Once she started on the subject, she kept on talking about her children: their studies, habits, likes and dislikes and how pretty and handsome they looked. She smiled often, and didn't stop till the bill was paid by Siddharth. She had the choicest of dishes — the ones she adored — and dessert of Cassata ice cream, and rounded it with a cup of espresso. Maybe, both were aware that it was their last meeting.

When the waiter left after getting a generous tip, her fingers clutched one another nervously. He knew she wanted to say something.

"Siddharth, is it not possible—" she fumbled for words — "can you not come back to me — and — your children?"

The stream of tears broke through the barrage of controls she had been operating for the last one hour.

For an instant he felt like chucking his job, kicking Lata out of his life and going back to his wife and children. But he was already over the bridge, and it was not possible to negotiate the rough terrain again.

He wiped her tears, caught her hand, and slowly led her out of the hall; the waiter kept the door open for a long time, and bowed deferentially. Once in the corridor of the Connaught Place, she was composed, and he let go her hand.

"Can I drop you anywhere?" she asked, her throat hoarse.

Overwhelmed, he simply shook his head, touched her lightly on the temple, and hurried away.

Later, he had wept and wept in the central park.

Lata had been furious with him for not insisting on divorce. "What sort of a man have I staked my life with? With all your strength, you are a useless man when it comes to the crunch."

He didn't defend himself, and refused to enter into any dialogue with her on the subject.

"I'm not going to live in adultery with you all my life." She warned.

"It's your choice."

"If you can't do it, I will go to Delhi and drill some sense in Ambika."

"If ever you do so, I'll never marry you." His tone was menacing. Three months later, the divorce papers arrived signed by Ambika.

"I underestimated you." Lata smiled, and added, "If I were in her position, perhaps I would not have signed the papers."

She looked at him, and asked, "Are you unhappy?"

"Breaking away from your children and wife whom you have loved since the first year of college is not easy?"

At night, he didn't make love to her.

"Sometimes, I feel that you and Ambika are of the same kind I am the odd one," Lata said.

Ambika's ma had protested against letting Siddharth get away without any struggle, and without any alimony. "There is no point of holding on to him if he does not love me anymore. For us, he does not exist now," she replied.

She had learnt that Siddharth and Lata didn't have any children of their own. Was it god's way of punishing them? However, she refused to let him visit the children. He had considered seeking legal remedy but shelved the idea. How could he drag her to the court after being so unfair to her?

Rain pelted down on the roof, and disturbed her thoughts. Siddhartha hated driving in the rain and especially at night. Worse, he was a rash driver and it worried her.

Why had she not found another partner? In the initial flurry of sympathy wave her friends had poured in large numbers, gradually, they left her to cope with her changed circumstances. For many years, she hated the male specie for being obsessed with its concupiscence unmindful of the consequences: how it affected the wife and children?

When the pent up anger subsided, she was in her late thirties and made sincere attempts to win the heart of someone – a colleague, friend or even a distant acquaintance. She decided to expand her circle, increased her wardrobe, chose friends who had a positive outlook to life and started going to the gym. At conferences, symposia especially those in exotic hill resorts or abroad, she started looking for unattached males. It surprised her that it was so easy to ensnare men. However, with time she learnt that men were not as inane as she had visualized, most of them had left their wives ensconced in the safety of their homes and were simply trying for a cosy night in the arms of a willing partner. Strangely, the only company she enjoyed was that of married men. She pined for the scent of a man in her bedroom, and in all her day reveries and dreams that man was Siddharth. Sometimes, she hated herself for remembering him; if he had found another partner so would she, and a better man than him. She didn't give up, she bided her time.

She was advised by her friends that the world was changing fast, men preferred women who were bold, and daring. For almost seven years she had struggled to find a suitable partner and in her early forties, she grew desperate. Her dresses turned more flamboyant, the décolletage became deeper and her visits to the beauty parlours increased.

At a seminar in Manali, she had a horrific encounter with a professor of Mumbai University; she narrowly escaped getting raped by him. It was her last attempt at finding a husband.

She was back in her old clothes, and old lifestyle and she was more at peace with herself. She acknowledged she was not lucky in love, and accepted the accompanying loneliness.

Both the children were good at studies and overambitious. Deep down in their hearts, they were apprehensive of the institution of marriage. Aditya was even more obsessed of economics than his mother, and Vidya, two years senior to him, was into computers, making intricate software. Ambika wanted her children to get married before thirty, especially Vidya. When she crossed the dead line, Ambika was worried and reproved both of them. "I will give you a year and no more. Find out suitable life partners or I'll force both of you into arranged marriages."

Circumstances took a different turn. Vidya bagged a fellowship at Cambridge and on return was so busy in setting up a complex security system for a multinational that marriage took a back seat. Ambika appreciated, and didn't pressurize her. When Vidya turned thirty four, it pressed the panic button. It was during this time that Aditya met Leena, fell in love and married her in a hurry before the delivery of their child. Vidya was going steady with David, an Australian and a senior colleague in the company. Ambika knew that Leena hated her and it was unthinkable for her to spend the retired life with her son. David was a stranger, almost like an alien. Both siblings were worried as to what would happen to their mother after her retirement?

Lata's death changed the perspective.

Vidya had some work at Chandigarh and met her father for the first time and instantly liked him. Her visits increased, and she got to know him better. She reflected on various aspects of his personality, which she and her brother had inherited from him. She was tall and healthy like him, and Aditya was slim and lightly built like mother. The more Vidya thought on the complex traits of her parents, the more she was convinced that they were a compatible couple. Only circumstances had parted them, and they had changed now. Lata was no more and both were at the end of their careers. When she confided this idea to her brother, he grabbed it.

"But you will handle it," he said. The only time he had met his father, he had disliked him. He couldn't forgive his father for making his mother suffer.

"Don't worry, I'll take care." She assured him.

But selling such an idea to their mother was not easy. "How dare you two think on those lines? Going back to that man who threw me out of his life on meeting that bitch?" She had rebuked them, and turned so fierce that both of them were scared.

"I know you two are worried about my invasion in your lives after retirement. Don't worry I'll never impose myself on you two."

Persuasive effort by the siblings for many weeks mellowed her anger.

"You still love him ma whether you admit it or not --- that's why you could never find a man for yourself? And the fact is that he also remembers you. And he is such a decent and graceful man --- I feel proud that I'm his daughter."

Ambika's hatred of him had intensified after the Manali contretemps for she squarely blamed him for putting her in soup. The siblings were slow, gave her lot of time to mull over her future, and considered bringing the two of them together as the greatest project of their lives. Vidya was able to prevail over Ambika's deep rooted prejudice against Siddharth by bullying and cajoling.

Little by little, Ambika swallowed her pride. The past shrouded in turmoil and confusion was clearer now, and she attributed the break- up to circumstances. "Is it necessary to waste away the rest of your life in loneliness nurturing your ego?" Vidya argued bluntly.

After ten long months, Ambika agreed to meet Siddharth.

Vidya had given the same treatment to her father and he too, unwillingly, conceded to the meeting. However, in his case the guilt complex was more pronounced. Vidya's warmth and affection finally overcame his resistance.

Ambika rose from the seat, her legs had grown stiff. She peered outside; the storm was in its full fury. She had tried Vidya many times on the mobile, and could not reach her. A week back, Ambika was lukewarm to the prospect of meeting Siddharth but now she looked forward to it. She walked over to adjacent room, and overheard Aditya pacifying his wife on the cell.

"Adi, as soon as the storm subsides, you can leave. Don't worry about me," Ambika told him. She looked at the clock, it was almost 9 pm.

This time she didn't wear anything special. No perfume, not even a lipstick. She had attended a meeting with Vice Chancellor in the afternoon. Today, she had snubbed one of the principals who was a known bully, and often indulged in vulgar jokes. She wondered from where she had got the strength to overcome her diffidence.

The swishing of the car in the driveway, and the flashing of its headlights alerted her. Aditya ran outside with umbrellas, and Ambika stood in the veranda. Vidya opened the driver's door and dashed inside, Aditya helped his father.

"What hell?" Siddhartha muttered. "I've never seen a night like this. But for Vidya, I couldn't have made it on my own."

In the dimly lit veranda, he glanced towards Ambika, and said, "Hello." She felt his tone was not as warm as she expected.

She led him to the lounge and made him sit on the sofa. He removed his jacket, and handed over to the servant instead of throwing it on a chair. In his grey trousers, crisp white shirt and sleeveless woollen cardigan, he looked smart and athletic. His familiar paunch was missing.

"I've spoiled your carpet," he said formally to her.

"It's OK, papa." Vidya answered. The servant brought coffee; Vidya had told her mother that he preferred coffee over tea.

Ambika observed he had grown thinner, and seemed to tower over his son when they walked in together. Instead of the tousled bunch of lustrous hair, the grey hair were well groomed, the nose appeared thicker and ill placed over his features, and he carried the air of sadness around him with dignity. His movements and general demeanour was slow, reflective, and not impulsive. He had also lost the mischievous smile flickering on the lips that had first drawn her to him in the college. She didn't seem to know this man, he was almost a stranger.

There was an imperceptible sign between the siblings, though it didn't escape Ambika. Aditya left the lounge; humming a tune, Vidya casually rose after a few minutes, placed her arm warmly around her papa and disappeared.

"I have been waiting for the last four hours," Aditya shouted at Vidya. "Do you take 12 hours to reach here from Chandigarh?"

"He didn't want to come." She explained. "It took me over four hours to convince him."

"Why?"

"Guilt complex. He felt he was having the best of both worlds."
"There is no doubt about it -- but I didn't know he had a heart!"
"Stop being contemptuous - he has a much better heart than yours! For the last four hours you must have been worried only about your Leeni."

The exchange between the two was interrupted by Ambika who had missed nothing.

At the dinner table, Aditya excused himself. Confused, Siddharth inquired if he had a date.

"He got married six months back - his darling Leeni is waiting for him." Vidya clarified, and smiled impishly.

"Oh!"

Aditya shook hands, and left. All of them had escorted him to the gate. Ambika looked up; the sky was clearing though the pale moon was still surrounded by white clouds.

His departure had an unsettling effect, as if a pleasant ride was jolted by a sudden break, disturbing the rhythm. When Ambika didn't volunteer to clear the air, Vidya elucidated. "The decision not to invite you was Aditya's."

"But why?"

As soon as he had blurted out the words, Siddharth realized it was a foolish question. "How stupid of me?" he muttered, and smiled for the first time.

But it didn't relax the atmosphere. The dinner was insipid, and the table- talk rather drab.

When they returned to the sofa, Ambika made an effort to cheer him up, and said, "Vidya makes excellent Café Latte - her boyfriend presented her two large packets recently."

The coffee was invigorating, and they talked and talked of her boyfriend. Ambika learnt many new things about the young man.

At the first opportunity, Vidya slipped away to her room.

"When is she getting married?" Siddharth asked.

"End of Feb," she said.

Absent-mindedly, he nodded, and looked at the clock. It was past eleven.

"Do you sleep early?" she asked.

"No, I'm a little tired."

He rose.

Suddenly, he asked, "Isn't this clock the same one given by Parshant on our first marriage anniversary?"

She nodded. She had thrown the clock twice, and both the times Vidya had retrieved it from the rubbish. "If you don't like it, I'll keep it in my room and take it with me after my marriage," she had said. It connected her with the few happy childhood memories she treasured.

Vidya returned, and looked at both her parents wondering whether they had made any progress or not. They needed to be pushed together forcibly, she thought.

"I'll like to rest." He looked at his daughter.

"Of course," she replied, picked up his small briefcase, and affectionately caught his arm, and moved to her mother's room.

He hesitated before the spacious master bedroom.

In one glance he saw the raw silk bedspread with a maroon border, the cream coloured pedestal lamp throwing diffused white light, and a big bunch of red carnations on a side table adjacent to the bed.

"Is there a guest room?" he asked tentatively. He felt the loosening of his daughter's hold over his arm. Without a word, she moved ahead, and opened the door to Aditya's old room.

"It smells of economics —." She made a face.

"Once upon a time I was used to it." His spontaneous comment confused her, and she looked up at him.

"If you need anything, I am in the room opposite," she said. He noticed that the warmth in her had evaporated giving way to almost apathy. She wished him good night, and went to her room.

Ambika was just behind them when they left the lounge. When they moved towards Aditya's room, she turned back, walked towards veranda and sat down in the damp wicker chair. The pain she had buried deep in the recesses of her heart reappeared. "Why do I hope?" she murmured to herself. Tears swelled her eyes.

It was again pouring down in torrents. She remembered that the Met department had predicted that it would be a cloudless night.

She felt the long arms of her daughter around her. With her cheeks pressed against her mother's, Vidya whispered, "Give him sometime, ma."

■■■

Waiting

"Where the hell is the remote?" Sanjay Misra bawled at his wife. Leela slowly walked in from the kitchen, lifted the morning paper, handed him the TV remote and chastised him. "You are incapable of doing anything."

At least half a dozen times in a day he yelled for the remote because he knew his wife disliked his watching the movies and purposely misplaced it. She was fond of hearing the bhajans; it irritated him. "What has God done for me?" was his stand.

None of the children were with them. Three sons and the daughter were in the States. The old couple, in their early 80s, snapped at each other whenever something went amiss, which was most often the case. They'd once looked forward to the letters, e-mails, telephone calls and visits from the children, with the passing of years they realized their relationship with the children had withered away and they were chasing a mirage; they were no longer a part of their lives.

After every visit, the sons promised they'd ring once in a fortnight and the daughter would hug them and whisper, "I will e-mail every week." They kept their promises for a month and then subsequently forgot. Even now, a call from USA caused a ripple in Leela's life and she would jump up enthusiastically but the duty call deepened the void in their lives. Sanjay was immune to any messages from abroad. The grandchildren were worse in their attitude. The old couple did not have happy memories of their only US visit and they were never invited again.

Before retiring as Joint Secretary in the Ministry of Social Welfare, Sanjay had bought a flat in West Delhi and later shifted to a DDA flat at Saket. They hailed from Varanasi and had no relatives at Delhi. Over the past two decades, some of his friends had died and the others stayed with their children rather far off. They communicated only on the New Year.

The old couple did not suffer from any major chronic illness but age was catching up. His wife went for evening walks; he abhorred the practice and for the past many years had settled for stationery cycling. Their movements were slow; any physical activity was a torture. Sanjay's interaction with the neighbours was minimal, nothing beyond raising the hand. A gesture of hello and goodbye, coupled together. Leela visited Mrs. Veena Saxena, a schoolteacher, and spent some time with her.

Life was a drag, a burden. Sanjay and Leela had talked and talked of the past: their romance in college, the years before the children invaded their lives, their growing up, the joys and sorrows they had shared in the company of the kids, their going abroad and their marriages -- and exhausted themselves. Now they had nothing more to talk about. Sometimes an oppressive silence filled the room and it frightened them.

Though he had a Maruti Dzire, he had lost the confidence in driving; a driver was difficult to get and there was no place to go to. He buried himself in the company of books and newspapers; and when his eyesight started failing him he turned to TV. It was an escape for Sanjay and he lived in that world though half the time his mind wandered back to the past. The moving images on the screen were an assurance that life continued to move. Nothing touched him. The news of elections, the change in the government, the turmoil in middle east, the murders, rapes, the terrorists' bloody attacks or the movies. Sanjay flipped the channels and occasionally dozed off while watching HBO or Star Movies. Despite the noise of TV and the bhajans, an oppressive stillness prevailed in the house.

"What are we waiting for?" Leela whispered to her husband, once. She was aware of his answer, fortunately, he did not reply.

One day, Leela excitedly informed him that the Saxenas were going to Kanpur to attend a marriage and in their absence Mrs Saxena's niece was arriving to take the civil services examination.

"Veena wants us to keep an eye on the girl," Leela told her husband.

"What does that include?" Sanjay was wary of the ways of the world and invariably exhibited his skepticism.

"Nothing," Leela said and shook her head disgustingly. She disliked her husband's pessimistic approach. "The girl is from Roorkee and would need a little assurance -- she has never been to Delhi. She is a big independent girl and would manage her own food." Throwing him a deprecating glance, she said, "You don't have to do anything."

Sanjay heaved a sigh of relief.

He was surprised to see a tall, fair, delicate girl walk through the door one day. "Hello, Uncle. I'm Neha."

She looked attractive when she smiled. With her pleasant disposition and chirpy temperament, Neha charmed the old man. During the next two days, she made it a point to spend 10-15 minutes with them and the couple looked forward to her visits.

While asleep, Sanjay was disturbed by a scream; the yelling of "Help, Help," pierced through the night. The shrieks had come from the ground floor. Sanjay thought of Neha, grabbed his wife's walking stick and rushed downstairs shouting at his wife that the girl was in trouble. His frail legs were suddenly charged with energy. He found the door was open and he shouted aloud, "Neha, Neha where are you?" He heard a muffled sound emanate from the bedroom and he rushed in that direction. He found two men in the room. The younger one was wrestling with Neha and trying to prevent her from bellowing and the other was struggling with the steel cupboard locker.

"You bastards!" Sanjay shouted and wielded the stick and bashed the head of boy on the bed. He slumped and Neha jumped free. The other man at the cupboard was taller and stronger. He took out an eight- inch knife and lunged at Neha. Sanjay tried to hit him also in the head, misjudged and instead hit his shoulder. The man turned, and whacked the old man. Sanjay sank to the floor. The man stabbed the girl once and was about to do a repeat when he heard noise at the main door. In a trice, the man picked up the boy, opened the door leading to the street and disappeared.

When Leela arrived with help, Neha was in a pool of blood. Sanjay recovered from the shock, but Neha had to be rushed to Batra hospital. The case was reported to the police.

Neha was in the hospital for two days. Sanjay was transformed. He was bubbling with vitality: driving from the residence to the hospital and back in his car, administering medicines, consulting the doctor or the nurse. And patting her hand, he told her that she was a very brave but stupid girl for having opened the door to strangers in the night.

He was by her bedside in the morning when she opened her eyes, and prepared tea and offered to her. She saw the bandage on his arm and smiled weakly at him. "Thank you, Uncle, for saving my life."

He was apologetic for having missed the head of the second thief that had led to Neha's stabbing.

"Oh, come on, Uncle, you were great. You risked your life for my sake. But for you, I might have been dead."

Sanjay smiled and was pleased with his heroic effort.

On the third day Sanjay and Leela brought her to their home, nursed and pampered her. In the mean while the Saxenas extended their visit.

Sanjay explored the British Council Library and brought books on history and discussed them with her. Leela hovered around with a glass of milk or a cup of coffee. Sanjay forgot to switch on the TV and Leela gave up listening to bhajans. Once, when the elder son called at dinner time, Sanjay said, "We are very busy." and hung up the phone.

Those few days fled on airy wings and Saxenas arrived on the tenth day apologizing for the delay. Neha made it a point to spend some time with the Misras on some pretext or the other. They got so attached to the girl that on the day of her examination both of them went to the temple and prayed for her success as they used to for their children.

Before leaving for Roorkee, Niha hugged the old couple. "I will always be grateful to you both," she said with tears in her eyes. "And I'll e-mail you every week."

They talked and talked of Neha and the incident of that night for many weeks. When they read her e-mail, it lit up their lives for a few days. But once again their lives were engulfed in darkness as if someone had switched off the mains. Their lives were an eternal wait.

Waiting. Waiting, for something to happen.

Anything to happen.

■■■

Sibling Complexities

Varun looked at his elder brother Akshay and his wife, Reva, walking together towards their seats after blessing the newly engaged couple. Tall and fair, Akshay carried himself with dignity; his every movement was premeditated and gracefully executed. Reva, attired in a long evening sleeveless dress with a slight décolletage, looked ravishingly beautiful as she leaned coquettishly on her husband. They made a handsome pair as they smiled at each other. Twenty- one years in the Indian Foreign Service had given the duo a suaveness that was not easy for others to emulate. A twinge of jealousy flared in Varun. Akshay was ambassador to Peru whereas he was still a struggling major trying desperately to hold on to the army. The rebel in him had got him in trouble repeatedly. Recently, he had been involved in a case of physical assault on a Colonel and was apprehensive that he may have to face another court martial though he did not permit his dark future to cloud his demeanour during the marriage of his youngest cousin (the bride).

After the engagement ceremony, Varun searched for Sheila, his wife, and found her gulping golgappas with her sisters. Endowed with striking features, a more than generous bulge, dusky complexion, she was smart but lacked the style and ease of Reva. All male eyes were riveted at Reva, and chased her all over the lawn. Varun walked over to his wife and was received warmly by his sisters-in-law.

Varun's antenna alerted when Akshay and Reva along with some relatives, passed by discussing about his exploits in the army. A distant cousin commented, "Oh, you can be sure if Varun is in Southern Command, the army will be at war there." Akshay made a cryptic remark, and everyone burst in hoots of laughter including Reva. Satish, his youngest brother, had vainly tried to defend him.

Varun coloured and Sheila placed her hand on his arm trying to pacify him. His eyes never left Akshay and his wife throughout the evening; he avoided them and remained protected in the safe haven of his wife and her sisters. Suddenly, he saw Reva collide with someone. The wine glass crashed down, and the drink splashed on the sari of a guest. "Sorry," she muttered, and apologized.

"You alcoholic bitch!" The woman hissed as she tried to brush away the stains with a tissue paper.

"What the hell do you mean?" Reva shrieked. The husband of the lady jumped in the fray and also abused her. For an instance, Akshay was at a loss to comprehend the situation, and then walked over leisurely with a wine glass in his hand. He was surprised to find Varun scolding the woman's husband, his hands on his collar. The host rushed, and tendered apology restoring peace and order.

Akshay escorted his wife to a sofa. Later, Varun noticed Reva helping herself to some more wine, and it confused him. Hurriedly, he sought out Akshay and pointing his finger towards Reva requested him to intervene. "Stop her; she is out to make a fool of herself again?" Perhaps, his tone had an edge of rudeness, and it offended Akshay. He had also been piqued by Varun's physical assault on a guest tarnishing the family's image.

"She knows how to hold her glass — you better mind your own business." He paused, and added, "And control your lousy temper."

In a way, Akshay was right. Everyone talked of the incident and labelled Varun a hoodlum; the misbehaviour of the woman and her husband was forgotten. Varun had overheard about it, and felt sheepish. On spotting his mother he wanted to clarify his stand when she told him to keep his trap shut.

"Varun, sometimes you should learn to obey also!" Her voice was chilly, the face pale, and her eyes were aflame. "Rebelling, rebelling, all the time!" She shook her head furiously and walked away.

Humiliated, he went back to his wife.

The seed of rebellion in him was planted by Akshay, Varun pondered later in the warmth of his bed as the images of the past flooded him. Papa was busy in setting up a Hero Honda showroom in West Delhi, and ma ran the house with an iron hand. A physics lecturer at Miranda house, she checked their homework, scolded and abused her sons if they did not do well in science or mathematics, and all of them loathed her favourite subjects. Unable to take it beyond a point, Akshay reacted one day and threw away the algebra book, and in turn was hit by his mother. Insulted in presence of younger siblings, his blood boiled, and he left the house and threatened never to return. He had spent the night at his uncle's. It was then that papa, who generally did not interfere in family matters, interceded. The science stream was discarded and Akshay opted for arts. He became Varun's idol and hero.

Nicknamed as `Malohtra Devils', their daring pranks were the talk of the school and neighbourhood. They cycled in the market with closed eyes, deflated cycle tyres of boys they did not like, broke the window glass panes of their neighbours, smashed the street lights, plucked all the flowers from the nearby gardens and locked their teachers in the staff room. Under Akshay's protective care, he was unassailable. And they opposed their ma on every front. Varun remembered those days with nostalgia. Satish was their opposite; docile and introvert, and was not a party to their escapades.

But once Akshay joined History (Honours) at St. Stephen's, he reversed the gears and became obedient at home and college. It was as if a new Akshay had arisen from the ashes of his recklessness; his behaviour was impeccable. Initially, Varun felt it was play-acting on part of his elder sibling, and he would be his old self soon, and together they would again indulge in mischievous acts. 'Chameleon', 'turncoat', and 'hypocrite' were the euphemism used by Varun for Akshay in his own private world. When the weeks rolled to months and a year slipped by, he realized it was for real. He missed Akshay's company and camaraderie. However, Varun did not change, and on the contrary became more truculent as if to make up for Akshay's absence in his exploits. Unable to rationalize the situation at the tender age of adolescence, he had gone off on a tangent and felt that Akshay's turning a new leaf was tantamount to a breach of faith: he felt cheated and betrayed. The little ulcer spread its tentacles all over his body suffocating him and warping his view of life. Barely in his early teens — he was hardly fourteen or fifteen — he held his elder brother responsible for all his failures. The more he ran into thick of trouble, the more he blamed him. Perhaps, he might have been able to handle it in isolation, but ma's scathing criticism of him and lavishing rich praise on Akshay when it was not even due, compounded the problem and it had made him hate his elder brother, the one who had been his idol throughout his childhood.

His performance in the Board was better than his elder brother and he joined Sri Ram College for Commerce (SRCC) in Eco (Honours) against the wishes of papa who had wanted him to go in for commerce.

Akshay became ma's darling and Varun her bête noire. Once in a while, papa supported Varun when ma went overboard; such instances, however, were few and far between. It was a bad year for Varun. Without the patronage of his elder brother, he was unable to make any friends in the college. To impress his class fellows, he tried his old school tricks, but they misfired and he had to cut a sorry figure apart from receiving the reprimands of the college authorities. At home, ma made his life miserable, now she had the tacit support of Akshay.

Everything around grew so stifling that he wanted to escape the claustrophobia. Army was a handy escape. Some of his school friends who had gone to the army talked endlessly of the glorious service, and Varun got carried away. When he informed of his future plans at home, there was a howl of protest from ma though papa had supported him. "Why not? We should have a General in our house!" Papa did not have the time, neither the sensitivity to appreciate his second son's weaknesses. Ma was sharp and understood him, unfortunately, opposing her had become a part of his nature. Akshay knew him well and was fully aware that his rebellious and short -tempered nature was not suited for the army, but he had dismissed the whole thing summarily. "It is for you to decide," he had said and walked out of the room.

Now in retrospect, Varun had the uncanny feeling that by being non-committal, actually Akshay had pushed him to the army. Maybe, he had the perspicacity to foresee that the regimentation in the army would destroy Varun and then he would be the cynosure of his parents. It was not incidental that Akshay had benefited the most from papa's will.

Akshay and Reva went through the painful process of marital adjustments, and sometimes were at loggerheads with each other. She was impulsive like the rain in August whereas he would plan for December in March itself. Bubbling with zest for life, she had clicked with Varun, and they enjoyed each other's company. (In those days he was posted in Delhi where as Akshay was away on training and Reva had not given up her advertising job at Nehru Place.) Once, he had indulged in the impertinence of asking her, "What do you have in common with Akshay?"

"Love." She had laughed.

"Really?"

"Of course!" She snubbed him.

That incident had snapped the ease in their relationship and it was never the same again, not even after his marriage.

Varun tried to rationalize the incident of the evening. Maybe, Sheila was right when she explained to her sisters that he transported little things of life into a war situation where he was at his best. He had earned glory in Kargil war, and later done commendable work in dealing with the terrorists. He felt there were laurels to be won in the war and wanted to get away from a peace- situation where he felt redundant.

His personal explanation was over simplistic. He hated the army for the bullying and servility expected of the junior officers. He was repeatedly advised to be of thick hide and get attuned to the army culture; somehow he had grown hypersensitive and lost self-control on a flimsy pretext. Though, a few inches shorter than Akshay, he had the strength and the build of a wrestler. In his anxiety to control the situation, he indulged in physical violence without being conscious of it.

God had not been fair to him, he thought. In childhood, papa felt that he was more intelligent than Akshay; ma did not agree and sided with her elder son. Satish could not make it to the college and joined father's business. As Varun continued to get involved in one imbroglio after another in the army, his parents pinned their hopes on Akshay. At one stage Varun thought of chucking the army and joining the family business, the resistance had come from Satish and his wife. The business was not doing well, and papa was apprehensive about Varun's volatile temperament. On being pestered, the old man had said, "At present, I want someone balanced and steady. Not someone who is in the habit of lighting a fire in a glacier."

That had decided the issue. He had no animosity towards Satish or his father. He understood.

But Akshay's polished bearing and refined manners discomforted him. It made him look philistine. Akshay's lean body, the long handsome face, and the superlunary air about him twisted his stomach in a dozen knots.

Varun realized that over the last twenty years of marriage, the blunt edges of discord between Akshay and Reva had smoothed out and they appeared to be now a compatible couple. With a son in the final year at school, they projected to be a happy family. Ma gloated when she talked of the higher diplomatic circles in which Akshay and his pretty wife moved, and it disturbed Varun and Sheila's equipoise. Varun was not deluded by the superficial laughter of the couple and was in the habit of exploring the undercurrents. He had met them on hardly two- dozen occasions after his marriage and that too for brief spells. Two years back he was able to trace some rift between the two and it had made him immensely happy. For the cousin's marriage, Akshay and Reva had arrived by different flights in the morning, she from London and Akshay from New York. Since then, they had been lukewarm to each other. When he had passed their room in the afternoon, he had overheard the two shouting at each other. The bone of contention was the dress she had to wear for the engagement ceremony. Ma wanted her to be attired in a sari, and she had flouted it. "How can she order me to wear sari?" She had screamed at her husband. "Am I not old enough to know what is good enough for me?" She had her way. "But perhaps my wife cannot have her way," Varun said to himself.

The whole night he was disturbed and fell asleep only in the early hours of the morning.

Handing him a cup of tea in the morning, Sheila went away to meet the newly arrived guests. Worried about his future, Varun was sipping tea when Reva walked in with a cheerful smile fluttering on her lips.

"Hi! I came to thank you for the help you rendered me yesterday evening," she said, and took a sip from a tumbler full of tea. Dressed in a light pink satin nightdress with slits on both sides at the bottom, and a black sleeveless, buttoned cardigan, her every step and movement radiated youthfulness. There was no chair in the room, and Varun tapped the bed and asked her to sit down. For an instant, she hesitated. Varun was sporting a sleeveless T-shirt and his rippling muscles were exposed. She pushed the blanket away, and made some place for herself.

"I am told that you took another rap from ma and your bhapaji (elder brother) because of me."

Casually, she crossed her legs, placing the right leg on her left, and he could see the lower region of her thigh. Her sensuality was electrifying.

"I am used to it," he said taking his eyes away from her curvaceous legs, and looking directly at her.

"For once, my husband was right. I can handle the glass well. Actually, I had stumbled on the uneven lawn." She flashed a smile at him. In a moment, she turned grave and added, "Sometimes, your bhapaji can be very difficult."

He nodded, and said, "I know."

"No, you don't."

The sharpness in her voice took him by surprise. Her eyes wandered over the room and rested on the facing wall where an old painting managed to cling to the wall in a skew position though one of the two nails on the wall was missing. "We all hang on to, whatever the little we have. But why?"

He could see the tears lurking in the corners of her dark eyes. He placed his hand on her bare arm trying to mollify her.

"His every action is very well planned." She turned her head and looked directly at him. "Yesterday, you were the first one to react — it's your natural impulse to come to the help of someone who needs it. But your brother is the last one. During the time he left his seat and walked up slowly to me, he would have thought out all the consequences, which could affect his career, his image, his life, their pros and cons and then decided to take the plunge."

"You are stretching it too far."

"No, I am not." She had never been critical of her husband earlier. "It is the precise assessment of Akshay."

She controlled herself and attempted to smile again. "Should you not learn something from your brother? Look, where he is and where you are?" She paused and added, "Or where you will be??"

He put up a brave face and grinned. "Thank you for your advice, but maybe, it is too late."

"I hope not." Her voice turned husky. She rose, touched him lightly on the arm, and went away.

After the pleasant encounter with the pretty sister- in- law in the morning, Varun felt more at ease with himself. When he met Akshay and Reva over lunch in the lawn, he was a little surprised to find them laughing together, their fingers entwined. He smiled at Akshay, and said a 'hello' to him.

"Come, come, Varun." He placed his arm affectionately over his shoulder trying to make up for yesterday's altercation. "Reva, do you know that Varun and I were great buddies in childhood." He went on to detail some of the exploits of the school days. Reva nodded nonchalantly, and slipped away to get another puri.

Carried away by the ruminations of the previous day, Varun suddenly asked his older sibling, "Why did you push me to the army?"

Surprised, Akshay reacted fiercely. "What nonsense are you talking? If I remember it correctly, I told you to decide for yourself."

"But you were fully aware that I was not suited for the army — you could have stopped me."

"You seem to have lost your head. Then you would have blamed me for not allowing you to do what you wanted to?"

Varun realized he was acting childishly; after all, Akshay was not privy to his introspections. Flustered, he turned to go but Akshay caught him by the arm.

"Why do you behave in this way?" Akshay asked angrily. His other hand which held the plate trembled slightly. "Are you jealous of me?" He glared at Varun, and added, "I have been watching you for the last many years. I didn't want to say it but it is a fact. You are jealous of my job, my status, my good looks, my wife, son — everything."

"Oh, shut up!" Varun shouted at his brother for the first time in his life, and left abruptly to avoid an ugly situation.

Reva did not like Varun's angry face as he brushed past her and dashed off to his room. She went up to her husband, and inquired.

"I have told Varun the truth that he is jealous of me."

She refused to believe her husband. Reva was fond of her brother- in- law; knowledge of his latest episode in the army had turned her more sympathetic towards him.

Varun was infuriated and gnashed his teeth: a storm raged within him. "I should have knocked down the bastard," he muttered. He threw his coat, gulped half a Bisleri bottle and poured some of it on his head. It took him a long time to control his heart beat. Eventually, he closed his eyes and dozed off.

Sheila woke him in the late evening. She had been sent on an errand by her mother- in- law and learnt about the quarrel from one of her sisters.

"Why are you fighting with bhapaji? It is not going to help you tide over your army problems." She had spent the whole afternoon mending fences with her mother- in- law so that if Varun was thrown out of the army, at least he could join the family business. After her father-in-law's death, everything now depended on the whims of the mother-in-law.

"His very presence annoys me," Varun said bitterly. "He is like a cobra, waiting to bite."

Refusing to be drawn into any argument, she told him to get ready for the marriage dinner and the subsequent nuptial rituals.

The marriage festivities in the lawns of Taj Palace were pompous and loud. Heavy snowfall in the hills surrounding Shimla plummeted the temperature in the capital and it turned unusually chilly in mid December. Varun decided to stick to his wife, his fleeting gaze had spotted his brother and sister- in- law. Reva, accoutered in a red Kanchivarm sari with a deep cleavage blouse looked bewitchingly sexy. With a plate in her hand, she sauntered over to Varun saying a big 'hello', and exchanged confidences with Sheila. Akshay arrived a few minutes later and stood beside his wife. The two brothers glared at each other, and it made their spouses uneasy. Reva caught her husband's arm, whispered something to him, and the two strolled away.

The marriage rituals were initiated late in the night. Akshay was associated with some ceremonies as the cousin had no real brother, and he positioned himself just behind her and her parents. To protect the children from severe cold, ma asked Varun to take them home. He reversed the car in the parking lot and noticed Reva waving frantically at him. "I am shivering, I want to go home." She opened the car-door and slid next to him. She felt warm and cosy. Exhausted, she closed her eyes during the half an hour drive.

When he reached home, Varun carried the children to their respective rooms. On return, he found Reva was still asleep. "Get up Reva, we are home," he said. It had no effect on her and he shook her violently.

"I'm sorry," she said, and wriggled out of the car.

The biting wind hit her, and she trembled. Varun folded her in his arm as he walked with her. At the stairs, he helped her on each step. The warmth of his body was comforting to her. She fumbled on a step, and he picked her up, carried her to the room, and switched on the lights.

He looked at the room; it used to be his in school days. Except for the single bed now changed into a double one, there was little change in the setting of the room. The wardrobe, table, chair and the book rack were all recently polished. The beige coloured wall-to-wall carpet, the matching curtains, the brass table lamp with a maroon coloured shade, a TV, and DVD player were new acquisitions but the old familiarity of the place enveloped him. Her face pressed against his, her pouted lips pointing upwards, eyes half open, she was light like a feather, and he could feel her breath on his face. At that moment it flashed across him that during Satish's marriage, he had spent a night in this room with his wife. Slowly, he placed her on the bed; he felt her arms harden on his neck as if refusing to let him go. He looked at her flushed painted face, golden dyed hair, and fair mounds and gently disengaged her arms. He walked to the open door, switched off the light and stood there for a long time. Abruptly, he closed the door, turned the latch, and moved towards her.

Rubbing his eyes, when Varun awoke in the morning, he saw that his room was flooded with bright sunlight filtering through the window; it sparkled on the golden yellow satin quilt and breathed a new life to the gladioli in the vase. Sheila rose, smiled at him and brought him a cup of tea. Varun peeped through the window and noticed Akshay sitting alone in the garden. He went down the stairs and turned towards the lawn. Despite the pleasant sunshine, Akshay was feeling cold and uncomfortable and had wrapped his arms around his body. Varun noticed that most of his hair on the sides had turned white and there were prominent dark circles underneath his eyes. He looked tired, vulnerable, and ordinary. A wave of sympathy for his elder brother swept over Varun. He removed his shawl and gently placed it around his elder brother's shoulders and patted him affectionately.

■■■

Meera's Kitchen Garden

The very sight of vegetables assorted in crates, baskets or on the ground at the 'haat' thrilled Meera Sharma. Every Wednesday, the vast open land was converted into a vegetable market, and she made it a point to visit the 'haat' at least once a month. The bright red tomatoes, the purple aubergines, the pinkish onions, the dark emerald okra, the yellowish white cauliflower, and horde of leafy vegetables - spinach, 'maithi', mustard, 'bathua' and cabbage -- seemed to be smiling at her and competing with one another and whispering to her, 'Hi! Pick me up.' The collage of varied colours was a treat to her eyes as she walked around under the warm December sun. Whenever she was in a mood to buy fruits, she would have a servant beside her, but today she walked around trying to find out the rates of vegetables and purchased nothing. Meera lived in a sprawling government bungalow and produced bagful of vegetables in the kitchen garden most of which she sold through her gardener. She was here to find out how much the gardener had fleeced her?

Initially, Meera was not happy at Bhopal; in fact she was not happy anywhere. In the last twenty five years, her husband had been transferred to eleven stations in six states and she had moved along with him. Instability and insecurity were a part of her life. With no friends and relatives around, loneliness hit her hard. Often, she wondered why unlike other wives of technocrats and bureaucrats, she and her husband took more time to make friends. Why were she and her husband so critical of new neighbours and his colleagues? Having lost their bearings, they were unsure of themselves and felt uneasy with everyone. Only at Kolkatta, they had struck instantaneous rapport with a couple from the Railway Accounts Service, but it had hardly lasted a year or so as the couple had moved away to Patna. And Meera went back to reading fiction. But how much could one read books? Over the years, the books seemed hollow and meaningless far removed from reality. In early years of her marriage she wrote poems; with lack of encouragement, her creativity diminished.

The idea of developing the kitchen garden was planted by her only son (now studying at Regional Engineering College, Karnal) and it slowly germinated in her mind. One day, Dina Nath, the gardener had hinted that vegetables could be sold in the market. The temptation of extra money that she could use the way she wanted to, had encouraged her to act on it. It kept her wholly occupied. Getting the seeds or bulbs or saplings and fertilizer, and learning new methods through a friend who was a Reader in an agriculture university, was a part of the entire process she enjoyed. As soon as her husband left for the office, she dashed to the kitchen garden, walked around with the gardener instructing him what to do for next few hours. She learnt the art of preparing the beds, quantity of water required for different vegetables; and tended them with her own hands. When the leaves appeared for the first time, it exhilarated her as if she had created new life and shaped it. She felt a part of nature, a part of god. Usually, she maintained a low profile but when the garden was full of vegetables, she walked around with a little swagger. She fondled the vegetables, and sometimes when she was very happy even talked to them. She had tried her hand at the flowers and given up; they were too delicate and needed to be handled with more care. And there was no market for them.

Looking at the rows of cauliflower and cabbage or aubergines wrapped in green leaves, she was thrilled. One day, she realized to her own surprise that after her son had become independent and didn't need her, she had seldom felt so happy in last many years. The joy of plucking the vegetables, cooking them with her own hands and savouring the delicacies with her husband was a new kind of happiness she had not experienced before. It inspired a surge of creativity, and she again started penning poetry.

She had carved out a life of her own in which she was very satisfied and happy. Her husband was an upright officer and she was proud of him. Her only differences with him were in the area of finance. He controlled the purse, and gave her a fixed amount for running the house. By and large, she was indifferent to his salary hikes through promotions, increase in Dearness Allowance, Pay Commission reviews, or his frequent UN assignments to Middle East. He did not trust her as she was over extravagant. "If I knew you are such a miser, I would not have thrown away my college lectureship," she had told him repeatedly. By selling the kitchen garden produce, she supplemented her resources and indulged in luxury of buying cosmetics or purchased a sari once in a while. The sale of vegetables was a secret between her and Dina Nath; no one else was privy to it.

One day she rose at dawn and noiselessly slipped into kitchen garden. In early February, it was cool and she loitered around trying to fathom whether vegetables were asleep or awake. When light appeared, she noticed dew on the cabbage leaves and was lost in its beauty, tenderness and fragility. A slight touch of the finger turned the dew into water bringing a chaos in the otherwise serene ambience. Out of nowhere it occurred to her that it really didn't matter whether her parents loved her younger sister more than her - a thought that had rattled her throughout her youth and adolescence and sometimes even disturbed her now – or that she had kicked away her lectureship after marriage. For the first time she appreciated why William Wordsworth's bonding with nature transcended all other relationships.

Her real happiness centred around the saplings taking root, their growth and turning to vegetables and her sharing the boundless joy with her son on a visit; the money she made by selling them was of little consequence. But she had got addicted to the habit of selling vegetables in the `haat' and checking the prices and she liked it; the extra money was a bonanza that helped her in retaining her little financial independence.

Watching the vegetables neatly arranged at the 'haat' was a very different experience from that of growing them in the kitchen garden. Here the vegetables were in their prime, dazzling and seductive in their smiles trying to attract the customers. In their raucous voices, the vegetable sellers shouted the rates of their commodities trying to outdo their rivals. "Le jaoo, mitti ka bhao le jao." Take it, its dirt cheap. Some of the vendors played on the psyche of the customers and confidentially added with a twinkle, "This rate is only for you." Unconsciously, she visited a seller twice to find out the rate of cabbage, and was rebuffed by him. "You are wasting my time — I'm sure you don't have to buy anything."

Sheepishly, she turned away and on the rebound purchased some apples, oranges, and pears from adjacent hawker without even inquiring the price.

As she trudged along the road towards her home at Char Imli, she felt she had made a mistake in not taking the servant for the packet was a little heavier for her. Meera was a lightly built woman on skinny side; carrying a load of about 4-5 Kg over a stretch of one mile was too much of an effort for her despite the pleasant sun. She did not trust the old Fiat that often broke down and preferred to walk down the distance. She felt like going to a booth and calling her husband, PK Sharma, who was head of the telecommunication services in Madhya Pradesh, for a vehicle but changed her mind for he was sure to frown; he hated the misuse of government vehicle for domestic purpose. (There were no mobiles in those days)

"Meera – Meera!" A healthy, fair complexioned woman beckoned and embraced her. "My god, I can't believe it!"

Meera was perplexed, and could not place the woman attired in Kanji- warm sari, and loaded with gold.

"I am Indira Dubey — your cousin."

Unfazed by the lukewarm response, Indira informed that her husband had been transferred from Bombay to Bhopal as Divisional Engineer, Telecom six months back and she had joined her husband last Sunday. When Indira learnt that Meera was without a vehicle, she offered to drop her. Meera refused. Enthusiastic in projecting the filial bonds, Indra persisted, and Meera gave in. "What are govt. vehicles for?" Indira smiled at her cousin condescendingly.

"We are meeting after almost three decades," she said. "When was the last time we met? Oh yes, at Ritu's marriage! You should come to my house at Char Imli, have a cup of coffee, and then I'll drop you where ever you want me to."

Before Meera could explain that she also lived at Char Imli, Indira informed that she had lost her father three months back, and had tears in her eyes. Confused about her relationship with

Indira, Meera ascertained names of her parents, siblings and traced out the lineage. Indira was the daughter of a distant aunt from her mother's side who was not well off; her family did not mix with them.

Meera had never ventured towards the Type IV quarters in the Officer's Colony during last three years. The fully carpeted house, designer furniture, choicest of decoration pieces, imported chandeliers and three split air conditioners proclaimed aloud that the resident belonged to the upper crest of society. In contrast, her spacious lounge looked almost barren. When Meera commented appreciatively on a geisha doll from Tokyo, Indira praised her husband's aesthetics and continued to praise his hard- working nature. "He is darling of all the bosses," she added.

Meera learnt that her son was at the Indian Institute of Technology, Bombay, and daughter was doing Law from the Bangalore Law School.

"You know Meera — my husband loves and dotes on me. Look at the gold he buys for me!" She blushed slightly, her cheeks turning crimson. "I have a DDA apartment at Vasant Vihar exclusively in my name apart from two flats in my husband's name."

She recounted all the assets she had and after some time added, "I'm going to have a 'havan' in my house after a week. I'll invite you."

"Of course you would, my dear." Meera rose with a pronounced scowl.

When Indra was about to call the driver, Meera told her not to bother and disclosed that she stayed at Bungalow No1; everyone knew it was the residence of the General Manager, Telecommunications (GM). For once, Indira was dumbfounded and transformed; she started addressing her 'madam'. She kept on muttering "I'm sorry - but you should have told me."

Back home Meera was restless. Indira was at the top of the world: her husband adored her, she had money, health, and ironically even her children were doing better than her son. And here she was scrimping for rupees after selling the vegetables from the kitchen garden, and was so mean to cross -check whether the gardener was cheating on her or not. She felt small, puny and ashamed of herself.

Her husband had undergone a heart attack, and she was a patient of chronic bronchitis whereas Indira looked radiant and her husband—she had met him at a party a month back—looked at least ten years younger than her husband though he was actually slightly older. To what use was her husband's honesty, his uprightness? Wasn't god unfair?

What pained her most was the lift she had taken from the corrupt officer's wife? At Delhi, sometimes she was forced into circumstances where she had to take a lift from others though her husband as a Senior Deputy GM had so many vehicles at his disposal. But she had never felt such a stab in her heart after sitting in the Jeep today.

Her husband returned late from the office, skipped his evening cup of tea and sat down exhausted at the dinner table. Though in his late forties, he had aged substantially after taking over charge of the circle. His countenance was grave. He was extremely critical of the slow pace of work culture in the state. "All the time these officers are obsessed only about making extra money," he told his wife.

"Why don't you?"

The sharpness in her tone made him look up at her.

"Meera, we made our choices long back when I joined the service," he said and looked kindly at his wife. "And I'm grateful to you for that—you have helped me to adhere to my principles."

"But why are you so upset today?" He inquired. She told him everything, even her bitterness.

"Are you not mixing up issues?"

She was familiar with his line of arguments: Indira's children were more hard-working and intelligent than her son spoilt by her pampering, the Dubey genes and life style was better than theirs, therefore they had no health problems, and they had more money because her husband was corrupt. God did not figure anywhere. They had gone over these issues often; she didn't want to go through this again.

"May be," she said thoughtfully. "But it hurts."

Provoked by his wife, PK Sharma told Murthy, the Vigilance Officer (VO) next day to keep a watch over Dubey. At the closing hours of office, he called Dubey and advised him not to indulge in illegal practices. "It is not MTNL, Mumbai but Bhopal." He warned. "If you slip up, I'll not spare you."

At night, Dubey reproved Indira for talking loose. In next few meetings Meera was unusually cold to Indra and it scared her. Worried about the future of her husband, she kept surveillance on Meera's activities.

Three months later, on receipt of documents from Directorate, GM served a major charge sheet to Dubey in an old vigilance case. Sometimes later, Meera heard gossip through her maid servant that the entire colony was talking about her weekly sale of vegetables in the market. Gradually, she realized that she was being marginalized in gatherings, and no one approached or talked to her except Directors' wives.

Six months after Indra's first interaction with Meera, battle lines were clearly drawn. From the hushed undertones, it was open revolt: GM's wife was misusing government land, cultivating vegetables and selling in open market. It was downright corruption.

Meera was shocked at such an insinuation. How could those women who had known her so well for last three years stoop to such a level of meanness?

Murthy brought it to notice of the GM. He laughed it off. When Murthy showed him a ruling that produce from the government land could not be sold without giving a certain portion of revenue to the government, he turned serious. He talked to his wife and was relieved that she had spent her money on purchase of seeds, fertilizer etc.

"Have I done something wrong?" She was worried. He understood her sensitivity. "It's a small matter, dear," he said, and next day deposited the required amount in government accounts.

A couple of weeks later, Minister for Communications paid a brief visit to Bhopal along with Secretary, Ministry of Communications to lay the foundation stone of a Telephone Exchange. After the function, Secretary told GM about the complaints he had been receiving regarding sale of vegetables in the market by his wife. "Sharma, please tell your wife to stop this childish activity. It's embarrassing."

Sheepishly, GM nodded.

When he told this to Meera, her little world was shattered.

Meera stopped going into the kitchen garden, and the gardener was also banned to enter that area. The vegetables turned dry and rotted away; her kitchen garden lay wasted. Neither did she visit the 'haat' again. Within months, her zest for life withered away. Unable to find an outlet to her emotions, she felt stifled, and told her husband that she could not stay there any longer. The GM applied for a transfer to Delhi.

■■■

The Street Dog

Bow-wow! Bow-wow!

The bark startled him. Taken aback, Amit Khosla stopped in his tracks, and noticed a teeny-weeny dog yapping at him. He dismissed it with a shrug and started to move ahead, but the bark grew louder. From his tall frame of six feet and two inches, he observed that the animal had black spots, alert eyes, tongue hanging out, and dangling breasts. The bitch was so frail that he could even see its ribs. It stared antagonistically at him though he had not given any provocation. The lane was a short cut he invariably took from his residence in the Railway Colony for a walk on the Shanti path, Chanakyapuri, New Delhi.

Amit refused to react, and stood still. Initially, he was amused and smiled indulgently at the small mongrel; he grew slightly apprehensive when it showed its canine teeth. It flashed across him that about three decades back one of his cousins on being bitten by a street dog was given a large number of injections in the stomach.

The very thought of pricks in his tummy frightened him. He held his ground for he was aware that if he ran, it would pounce on him. Suddenly, the cur was quiet as if reviewing its decision. It scratched its underneath with its hind leg, and rubbed its side with filthy tongue. There stood the man, and the bitch trying to asses each other.

Except for the small eyes, everything about Amit was enormous: big face, thickset nose, large ears, round bald head, broad chest, bulging stomach, long arms reaching up to his knees and powerful hands. With his sheer presence, he could dwarf his opponents and steal a psychological advantage, however, the bitch refused to cringe, and instead glared at him.

He rapidly surveyed the street. Yesterday's rain had formed puddles at many places and he could not spot any stone nearby. About twenty yards ahead, he noticed a few shards of earthenware scattered near the boundary wall of a palatial bungalow. Keeping an eye on the animal, he slowly inched towards his goal. The bitch made up its mind, growled, and turned ferocious. He could see the flesh distort into thick lines on the upper portion of its jaw. It took a swipe at him. Amit stepped back, and shooed away the menacing brute. It again rushed towards him, and he jumped on the left. Fortunately, he had reached his destination, grabbed a broken terracotta piece and hurled at the bitch. Amit had represented his college as the opening fast bowler and was known for deadly accuracy, but he failed to hit the dog from such a short distance. He picked up a few more pieces, and threw them at the bitch; one of them hit the target. Barking shrilly, it disappeared from the scene.

Hurriedly, Amit reached the road, and looked back to ensure that the bitch was not following him. He wondered at his own stupidity for using the lane littered with garbage. A few more turns, and he was on the Kautilya Marg.

Amit had a knack of rationalizing situations; he could not comprehend why the bitch had created the ruckus. It had disturbed his poise though he was known for his cool temperament. In his fifteen - year stint at the Rail Bhavan, the headquarters of the Railway Ministry, no one had ever seen him in an agitated state. Whenever the crisis deepened, he turned more sangfroid. Nothing perturbed him, but today, he felt a little discomfort near his heart. He rubbed his chest hard; it did not alleviate the pain. He made a mental note to avoid the street in future.

His dislike of dogs was well known amongst his family, friends, and relatives. It was beyond him to touch or cuddle a dog; his whole body revolted at the contact. While on deputation to Environment Ministry (headed by Maneka Gandhi) where dogs were considered holy, he was unable to change his attitude though he was an admirer of the Minister. Even a discussion on the subject of dogs sent a prickling sensation in his body. The pets of some of his friends understood his body language, and reciprocated with a snarl when he entered their house.

His children were keen to have a pet, and Aarti, his wife, was not averse to it. Amit was scandalized at such a suggestion and put down his foot firmly. "Not in my home."

"You are not human." His son rebelled.

"There are millions in our country who need your love and care—shower it on them. Why on a filthy, lousy dog?" Amit argued vehemently, and lectured on the suffering of the poor, and helpless. No one took him seriously. The real reason, all the family members intuitively felt was his over fastidiousness to cleanliness. He was so finicky that it made others uneasy. His room, at office or home had to be spick and span, and everything in its proper place. A paper jutting out of the file, file not properly flagged and numbered or even a pin fixed improperly - he did not allow it to pass and reprimanded the officer. It was no different at home. Shoes out of place, necktie not in the proper hanger or a speck of dust on the dining table and it was sufficient to trigger the long harangue. Aarti had banned his entry in the kitchen for he was sure to find everything topsy–turvy. She was his opposite, and loved to languish in disorderliness.

A dog in Amit's house would have been nothing short of a disaster.

It was not a part of Amit's nature to look back in life and brood on his past. Today, after his interaction with the dog, he was in a reflective mood.

Two years before his retirement, he had just begun the formal presentation to the Railway Ministers and Board Members on the new initiatives taken to mop up revenue when a junior officer handed him a slip of paper. He read it and without batting an eyelid, continued and summarized the entire presentation of about an hour in twenty minutes. He informed the Chairman of the Board of his wife's sad demise and left the meeting.

Amit's marriage with Aarti was a failure; they were so incompatible in their habits, attitudes, likes and dislikes that they were at each other's throat even on a trivial matter. But they continued to be together for the sake of children. A fatalist, he accepted what god had ordained for him. The philosophical manner in which he had accepted the marriage, in the same way, he accepted Aarti's death also. He was not unduly shaken by it.

On reaching the roundabout, Amit turned towards Shantipath, and as usual, avoided the main road, and walked on the side-road along the embassy gates, parallel to the main road.

He remembered the isolated instance in his career when he had lost his temper while working as Additional GM, Western Railway at Mumbai. A major train accident had occurred fifty miles away from Mumbai. The operator in the control room was dead drunk and gave wrong signals. Rajdhani, and delayed Amritsar- Dadar express train running in the opposite directions were placed on the same track. Both the trains were not scheduled to stop at the station and rammed into each other. About ninety persons had died on the spot and hundreds of severely wounded were rushed to the nearest local hospital. The Cabinet Minister resigned creating panic at Delhi. Seeing the mutilated dead bodies, the critically injured children and women, Amit's blood boiled. PK Naidu, the official responsible for the accident was a short, lean man; he sat at one end of a bench feeling miserable. He had already admitted in writing that he was over drunk and had made the grievous mistake.

"Do you know what you have done, you rascal?" Amit roared at him when he encountered him. "Come, I will show you."

Dragging him by the collar, he had a round of the hospital where the dead and the wounded lay scattered.

"Look at these! You - and you alone are responsible for their death!" Amit shouted at him and threw him in one corner where some of the dead bodies were huddled on the floor. The junior officers intervened and carried away Naidu.

Amit Khosla's thought process was disturbed by the gentle horn of the pilot of a cavalcade of cars making entry in an embassy. Amit walked across the grass and was on the main road. The vast view of the green esplanade on both sides of the road flanked with flowering trees invariably filled him with joy, but today it failed to move him. The altercation with the dog had stamped his face with a permanent grimace.

Through the maze of his past, Amit recalled that in his adolescence, he was given to violence and could be brutal. When he was in eleventh class, an incident occurred that entirely changed his perspective of life.

Amit was thin and bony but nurtured the ambition to be the boxing champion. Joginder, the champion for last two years, and responsible for eliminating him in the very first round, ridiculed him endlessly and called him a 'rat'. Amit felt insulted, however, could do nothing about it and hated Joginder. The nick name continued to stick on Amit even though he had shot up in height in the final year. Noticing his son was going to pieces, Amit's father, a former wrestling champion of Punjab, took him to the gym every evening and also arranged for special lessons from Wilson, the school coach.

At the school championship in the final year, Amit again faced Joginder in the second round. Half the school was gathered to witness the fight. From the striking of the gong, Amit was on an attacking spree and surprised his opponent with powerful punches. He was so devastating that every hook was like a hammer. Unable to stand the continuous pounding, Joginder crashed down in the fourth round.

"Come on, face this rat!" Amit gnashed his teeth. Joginder rose and staggered. Two punches on the left eye, another on the head and he bled. He tottered and caught hold of the rope. A powerful left jab followed by three rapid hooks from the right on his eyes and Joginder swirled on the rope, was knocked out of the ring, and collapsed on the ground.

Amit jumped after him. Rivulets of blood oozed out of his opponent's face, eyes, nose and mouth. The referee stopped the fight. There were loud cheers for Amit, and boos for the fallen champion.

Joginder was rushed to the ICU of the nearest hospital and was declared critical. Against his wishes, Amit was forced by Wilson to accompany him to the hospital. In a few hours, Joginder's condition deteriorated and doctors lost hope of recovery. His mother was unable to control her fits. Seeing Joginder sprawled unconscious on the bed with half a dozen tubes and the pathetic sight of his wailing mother, changed Amit: he decided not to wear the gloves again. No one could dissuade him to change his stand. He went to the hospital everyday and prayed for Joginder. Miraculously, Joginder's condition improved on the fifth day and three days later he was discharged from the hospital. Later, Joginder and Amit became thick pals.

Amit accepted the scolding from his superiors and ignored their abusive overtones with nonchalance as if it was as much a part of life as taking dessert after dinner. It helped him to earn 'outstanding' entries in his dossier and his career graph moved faster than others. To him, self- respect and pride were misplaced emotions, and there was no room for sentimentalism in his career. He could take it even from his subordinates and the unions. But he never forgave them. Invariably, he was successful in handling any type of situation.

He never felt he was in a boxing ring.

Amit had the rare ability to forecast the impending danger many weeks in advance. His colleagues, in lighter vein, joked that he could sniff the crisis in the air. He felt the same uncanny feeling, but could not figure it out.

About six months back Amit Khosla had retired as Additional Member, Railway Board and was planning to shift to his own house at Noida soon. The first two months of retirement had passed comfortably; he was busy managing his finances and settling outstanding issues he had been postponing. But thereafter he was engulfed in vacuum; he realized retirement was painful. Earlier each pore of his body was vibrant, it was backed by the power of the chair he occupied. Now, he felt emasculated. Only two days back he had gone to the Rail Bhavan and experienced humiliation when a junior colleague had been cold to him and did not offer him a seat.

"Hello! Good evening." Someone accosted him. He looked up and noticed Pamela Watson, an old acquaintance of Aarti, smiling cheerfully at him. On Saturdays and Sundays, Pamela jogged, and invariably met him. He made sure to be at his best: branded T-shirt, smartest pair of jeans, sparkling white Nike sneakers, thick white socks, a generous spray of cologne and a broad grin. Though he had been seeing her for the last three years, he had not gone beyond a 'hello'.

He smiled back, waved his hand and was about to move forward as usual, when she stopped. "Hi! You don't look well today!"

Dressed in a sleeveless black top, denim shorts, her long shapely legs looking unusually fair in the light of setting sun, she was a symbol of vitality. Though in forties, she looked much younger than her years. Her concern took him by surprise.

"I am fine, rather very fine. Thank you," he muttered and to prove her wrong, switched over to jogging. It exhausted him and he panted for breath. Perhaps, he was overdoing it and stopped for a while.

Suddenly, he realized he was back again in the middle of the same street where he had encountered the bitch though he had wanted to avoid it. Habits die hard in old age, he contemplated; they take over most of the activities.

Bow wow, bow wow.

Amit froze. He saw the same bitch run up to him from the end of the street and bark defiantly; its snarl fiercer than last time. Scared, he beat a hasty retreat. The mongrel was too quick for him and bridged the distance in no time. Amit ran for his life. The bitch made an attempt at his calves. He stopped and turned to face the animal, his heart pounding at two hundred a minute. The dog also stopped, and barked violently. The bitch moved in a semi-circle, preparing its strategy to take a snipe at him. In a trice, he felt, he was in the boxing ring. He had to fight it out. Everything in life was getting out of control; even the tiny bitch had the temerity to challenge him.

He decided to act.

With speed of lightning, he swooped down, caught the neck of the beast in his big hands and flung it away. It crashed down in a drain near the edge of the boundary wall of the bungalow. The bitch yelped and took time to recover and get out of the drain. It returned to face him again; its whine filled the air. Now, he was ready for the mongrel and kicked it with all the force. It gave a shrill cry that pierced through the approaching darkness. He heard the barking of many dogs round the corner. Near the drain, he spotted a thin rod, and walked through the muddy water and picked it. The bitch moved and he slashed down the rod repeatedly with all his strength.

The movement ceased.

A motorbike's light lit the street and Amit saw the dogs enter the street from the other end. They were the puppies of the bitch. He realised that the bitch was trying to protect them. His own ghastly shadow filled the street. For the first time in his life, he felt ashamed of himself.

The mo-bike rider slowed down to a stop, looked hard at the animal and said, "The bitch deserved it. It had attacked me twice."

Not getting any response, the motor- cyclist drove away. Amit threw away the rod.

The puppies surrounded their mother and ululated making the plaintive atmosphere more ominous. For sometimes, he stood in cold sweat, staring hard at the four puppies. Abruptly, he shooed them away, collected the bitch smeared in blood and filth and ran down all the way to his residence. Unlocking his Swift Dzire, he placed the bitch gently at the back seat and drove to the nearest dog-clinic.

The vet looked suspiciously at the man and the cur covered in blood and black mud; they made a loathsome pair. The creepy sight revolted the sensibilities of the vet; he turned his face away and told Amit curtly to leave his clinic. A little confused, Amit requested him to treat the dog.

"I don't handle street dogs," he said insolently.

Throwing his visiting card on the table, Amit thundered at the doctor. "It's my dog and is in a bad shape. Some scoundrel has lynched her, and I want you to give her medical attention."

Distrustfully, the veterinary doctor glanced at the card and Amit. He examined the dog and said, "I am sorry, but the dog is dead."

His voice was cold.

"Please recheck," Amit asked; his voice quivered.

"I am sure."

Amit looked at the bitch stretched on the table. The vet had to be right. How could such a puny creature withstand his onslaught? He requested the vet to look after the dead body and gave him sufficient money to meet the expenses. When he returned home, it had started raining.

The next day, he was surprised to see the four puppies at the gate. He could not face them and dashed inside. He kept a close watch on the movement of the puppies through his servant but did not have the nerve to come out personally. On the third day, the servant informed that the animals had finally left their post. For the next two days he was deeply perturbed. He refused to interact with any one and did not go for evening walk. Then, one evening, he went back to the same lane where he had killed the bitch. Near the drain, one of the puppies was crouched against the wall: lonely and miserable. The other three puppies were not traceable.

He picked up the helpless puppy and brought it home.

■■■

The Swing

Sheila felt drained after a fierce exchange with Akash, her eldest son based in London. Communicating with him had never been easy; he was a replica of Prabhat, her husband. Akash's cavalier attitude in handling the strike had infuriated her. Though he had apologized, she felt an acute pain in her chest. "Perhaps I am over doing it," she muttered. She picked up the receiver to send for the doctor but changed her mind. Instead, she had a cup of tea; it alleviated the ache. "Maybe, my time has come," she spoke aloud to herself.

She looked down at the lawn below and her face wreathed in smiles. Her grandchildren were playing in the bright sunshine. Some were frolicking with the ball and others were on the swing. Panoply of images, spanning seven decades of her life, fluttered across her.

She was hardly five or six years. Her happiest moments were the ones spent on the swing. Her elder brother was ten years her senior, she had no rapport with him. Her only playmate was Binoy, her class fellow, who turned up rarely. At the first opportunity, she scooted to the swing in the park at the back of the house. The swing was her friend, her companion. It was her own world, her bower of bliss.

She did not even allow Binoy to be included in it; he was there to assist but not a part of it. Seated on its wooden seat, she talked her heart out, the mundane things no one had the time to listen. Sometimes, she broke into a refrain she had heard her mother hum in the bathroom. When on the swing, she was seized by a frenzy; it gave immense strength to her frail legs and she wanted to explore newer heights.

One day, as she flew to dangerous heights on the swing she spotted her father staring hard at her in disbelief. His eyes popping out, his hands swinging frantically, he shouted, "Guddi, Guddi, stop." That was the day she had soared so high that she had touched the `neem' leaves for the first time and was ecstatic.

When the rushing cold wind hit her body she felt a strange sensation as if she had collected all the joys that the world was capable of offering. Her father's presence had ruined it all.

"No more playing on the swing," he ordered when he finally caught her hand. She escaped from his clasp, laughed and flung her arms around her mother.

"Oh, ma, I had a great time!"

Warned by her parents not to play on the swing, she defied it at the first available opportunity and sneaked to the park. The joy of being airborne and the feel of wind swishing against her body were too great to be missed for a trivial reprimand.

Generally, she jumped from the moving swing, ducked and crawled away from the side. Once, she was not quick enough and the wooden seat bashed against her head. She had four stitches and was threatened with dire consequences if she ever sat on the swing.

But the urge to be with the swing was so powerful that in the night, when the breeze rustled past the window curtains, she imagined that the swing wanted to whisper to her about the unknown mysteries of life and beckoned her to come.

Unable to control herself, she defied her parents after a few days. Fortunately, Binoy was already there. She told him to push her harder. She winged her way in the sky, her legs touched the 'neem' branches and she even dared to pluck a few leaves. It was evening time; the stars appeared in the sky. Initially, they were faint, but within a few minutes they sparkled.

"Harder Binoy, I want to touch the stars," she said. And her friend shoved with all his little might.

"More, more," she shrieked as she raced away, her heart pounding with joy. The thrill, the seraphic joy she felt at that moment was too deep to share.

Her irrepressible laughter at dinner made her parents suspect she was up to some mischief. However, they could not guess her secret. She treasured those moments for she never experienced such euphoria of wild abundance and freedom in life.

Later, in school and college, she had no time to play. She wanted to do better than her brother, who invariably bagged a position in the board or in the university; it therefore made it harder. Buried in her books and notes, she missed out on all the fun.

After her marriage, she settled down in the joint family in a palatial bungalow on the Aurangzeb Road in Delhi. In one corner of the bungalow, there was a small swing; it was usually occupied by the horde of children in the house. Once she made a deliberate effort to grab the swing, a three- year old toddler appeared from nowhere and got hurt trying to catch the iron chain of the swing. The teenage daughter of Subhash, Prabhat's elder brother, created such a ruckus that Sheila did not have the courage to sit on the swing even when it was unoccupied.

Six months after her marriage, her father- in- law collapsed after a heart attack. Within a year, Subhash cheated Prabhat of everything; they were literally on the road. Her husband's trusting nature and lackadaisical attitude to life ruined their future. Sheila took loan from her father, bought a sick textile mill and turned it into a profit venture. The business flourished and she diversified into new areas.

Despite being in her late 70s and after three heart attacks, Sheila had not lost her grip over the financial empire of two score companies spread in eight countries and many parts of India. Now, she operated from her 10- acre residence on the Delhi- Jaipur highway.

Short and petite, she still carried herself straight and with dignity; her mind was agile and sharp. "The old bitch is still breathing on our backs," was the general feeling echoed by the spouses of the children. Two of her sons had fled from Delhi but not from her control. They were all scared of her phone, which rang at odd hours, for she did not bother about the time lag. She called when they were at parties, or taking a bath, or still worse, when they were making love to their wives or girl friends.

The back-stabbing by Subhash left its indelible imprint on her personality. The children, like their father, believed in goodness of human nature and committed blunders. But she trusted no one in business matters. Not even her husband and children. At family celebrations, social gatherings or formal parties, her nerves were taut, her antennas alert, so that no one could double cross her. Even in the tender moments with Prabhat, her brain was focused on the agreements to be signed next week and the benefits that would accrue to her with a slight amendment of a clause.

The death of her husband was a sad turning point. She survived it by taking more interest in the business, expanding it overseas and taking a firmer control. Many a time Reema, her widowed daughter who stayed with her and ran the empire on her behalf, was exasperated with her mother and had to remind her that Akash was in early 50s and could take his own decisions.

"Let them breathe, ma," Reema pleaded.

Sheila was aware that she should let them lead their own lives, but the fear that if she did not exercise proper control the Prabhat conglomerate would split up in no time, forced her to continue.

Tempted by the bright December sun, Sheila left the office and strolled in the lawn, talking and laughing with her grandchildren. She buried herself in a wicker chair and went back to the past.

Her husband could not catch her thought process in business matters; she was far ahead of him. But he stole more joys in life, she reflected. A university champion in tennis, he preferred the tennis lawns to the long hours in office.

Sometimes, he disappeared in the mountains with his friends, tracking through the mountains and sylvan valleys. Her happiness was limited to business decisions — expansions, diversification in new areas and profits. She had missed out on the small pleasures of life, she thought. It was worse after Prabhat's death. She envied her daughters- in- law for their carefree attitude, irrepressible laughter and endless gossip over nothing. But Sheila never relaxed and she never sat on the swing.

However, the swing was always there at the back of her mind, nestled in one corner in which she peeped whenever she had time to introspect. A memory she cherished and shared with no one, not even Prabhat.

A chill descended on the lawn. She noticed that the evening shadows had lengthened.

"Maybe Reema is right," she whispered to herself. "It is time to let go." She looked at the swing for a long time and walked decisively towards it.

Sheila heard a noise at the other end of the lawn; the entire household was there. Arun, her youngest son, handed her a huge bouquet of roses.

"A very happy birthday mama," he said. Every one joined in the chorus. Moved by their warmth, she hugged them.

"Come ma, the guests are waiting for you." Reema caught her mother's arm affectionately.

"No, first I will sit on the swing."

She smiled as if she had taken the most important decision of her life. Kicking off her sandals, she sat down confidently on the swing and told the others to move away from its periphery. The relatives felt it was one of the whims of the old lady and resignedly accepted it. All except Reema who had seen the glint in her mother's eyes and noticed the spring in her stride when she had walked towards the swing.

Slowly, Sheila pressed her feet on the ground and pushed it, the swaying of the swing made her feel happy. She told her grandson to shove hard, but he obliged with a gentle push. It irritated her.

"It is enough ma," Arun said trying to dissuade her. But it was her day and she wanted to have all the fun. Not expecting any help from any one, she firmly stood on the seat, as she used to do when she was a child, and jerked the swing expertly with all her might.

Soon, Sheila was soaring in the sky and felt the frisson, the freedom she had not experienced for the last seven-and-a-half decades.

"I have been a fool, a real fool to have missed out on all this," she murmured.

She felt free like the wind, discovering new heights, unknown joys. Even at the peak of her power, when she was rated as one of the richest women in the country and interacted with the heads of some of the smaller nations, she had not felt so exhilarated.

She saw the mighty sun setting in the horizon and skeins of red, crimson and golden clouds envelope the western skies. She recalled that at the hour of twilight, she would tell the swing to rest, as it was time for the sun and everyone to sleep.

She wished to confide in the swing how she had spent 30 years without her husband. But the din of the voices down below disturbed her. She thought of something, it slipped out of her mind in the noise.

"Perhaps they are thinking that I have gone crazy." She smiled smugly to herself.

"Ma, ma, stop it," Reema screamed hysterically. "Have you gone mad?"

"Yes I have," Sheila shouted back and laughed like a child.

She had not laughed like this for years. She wanted to catch the stars, but she could not spot them. Her gaze scanned the sky; the last rays of greyish silvery twilight continued to linger in the sky holding the approaching darkness at bay. It disappointed her for she wanted to hold the glittering marbles. She felt the icy wind hit her and prayed for the stars to appear. Suddenly, she saw the evening star resurrect out of the white clouds just above her.

"Thank God," she whispered.

In seconds, the entire sky was fulgent with infinite stars. And then it flashed across her that she wanted to tell the swing that she trusted him, something she had not done for decades. Unaware that her left foot was close to the edge, she thrust herself forward for the last time in her effort to catch the stars, and slipped. There was a loud thud.

The empty swing continued to oscillate in the cold night.

■■■

Temporary Family

I am told that I was born on a cold January night when the Shimlaites shivered and cursed. The dark clouds had thundered and it had poured down heavily since early dawn. The chilly wind cut the flesh and made one turn blind. The wise men looked at the heavens, shook their head and said, "It's going to rain for 7-8 days." Rain starting on a Sunday, lasted at the least a week. The temperature dropped suddenly in the night and snowflakes glided down from the black sky covering everything in white. Roads were blocked, the pipes burst and the ambulance could not make it to our home. Getting the family doctor had not been easy. "What an unearthly hour to be born," the lady doctor had muttered throughout the delivery. Next day, looking at the mountains and the valleys swathed in snow, my old grandfather christened me `Hemanshu', a part of snow.

Except for the old man, the sprawling, rickety house was deserted; the other family members had gone to Solan to attend a marriage and could not return in the night. A death like loneliness pervaded in the house, often disrupted by my howling. That loneliness became an integral part of my life.

Without any sibling, I was lonesome as a child. Ma taught history at Lady Shri Ram College, Delhi and I was thrown in the lap of a nanny. My father was a Reader in mathematics department, Jaipur University and I met him during vacations or once in a month. Both of them refused to give up their jobs; and after initial bickering, decided to remain at their respective places, and I was bereft of an integrated family.

I grew up noticing my mother studying the calendar, calculating the casual leaves she could avail so as to spend the maximum time at Jaipur. Pressed for time, she scurried through packing, unpacking, dashed to the bus stand in a state of frenzy and prepared her lectures in moving buses or trains. And I hung on to her, staring at her in awe, and wonder. I realized that journeys were associated with meeting my father and looked forward to these visits. It was great fun to be with him. He wrestled with me, played cricket and later, taught me chess. I learnt the magic of numbers, was exposed to the physical laws of nature and the world of elements. My father had the art of turning most difficult things into interesting stories. Despite all his attempts, I felt a little formal with him. Almost like a stranger, or at the best a regular visitor; I could not penetrate the mysterious air around him.

Though obsessed with her career, ma took many years for the doctorate; most of the time I was alone at home and eagerly looked forward to her return from the college. Not even for an instant did I feel awkward or uneasy in her company. She lost her cool, screamed at me and sometime even bashed me. I accepted it. In contrast, my father showered all his love, gave me undivided attention, never frowned or scowled at me. I always found him cheerful and he laughed a lot. Initially, when I was young, I thought my papa was not real and pinned it on the limited meetings. As I grew older, I felt, perhaps he was not natural and only during my college days, it occurred to me that maybe, he was a little phony. Weren't fathers supposed to get angry with their sons?

With years, I could make out from ma's expressions when we were about to take the journey, grew familiar with the bus, and train schedules and on seeing particular trees, shops or houses knew that we were about to reach our destination. I could close my eyes and run through the entire route in my mind, both ways. Papa stood at the same place, leaning against the same wall, a stony smile on his face that I no longer liked. He welcomed us with a wave of his hand and then everything was predictable. His peck on my right cheek (never the left!), the warm hug, embracing his wife, the way we sat on his motor cycle, the remarks on entering the home ('now it is a home!'), the usual dinner with puris, the commonplace talk at dinner time, the same stories and the same maid for the last many years. Papa disliked any change in his lifestyle. Ma could not stand any routine for more than a few days and made it a point to force a change, however, unpleasant. No dinner or breakfast was ever the same. My home at Delhi (I refused to accept that Jaipur house was mine) was always in turmoil and I liked it that way. I was aware that papa was scared that she would upset the rhythm of his life and categorically told her not to interfere.

"Are you not tired of seeing the same positioning of the sofa for last ten years?" She questioned him, changed it and on return during the next trip found everything back to square to one.

"I am glad I am not staying here," she said.

I nodded my head giving my tacit approval. Papa noticed the movement of my head and simply ignored it with a smile. Feverish activity was ma's hallmark and she created it whether there was need for it or not. I realized later that it was necessary for her survival.

Till I moved to ninth class, I had no friend. I participated in group-activities but was unable to strike any rapport with anyone on individual basis. Partap, a new boy who had joined our section recently, was at loose end as he hailed from a mofussil background and other students looked down upon him. He stayed in the hostel and during the weekends went to his home at Meerut. His simplicity of character, warmth, and spontaneous laughter endeared me to him and we became friends. In the winter break, he invited me to spend a week with him.

At Partap's palatial bungalow, I was exposed to a different world. Spread over an acre of land, enveloped in tall eucalyptus and Asoka trees, it was an imposing white structure having three bedrooms on the ground floor and another four on the first floor. The guest room was occupied and I was to share the room with my friend. I was a little confused when I was introduced to all the family members. Partap had five brothers and six sisters; another three or four had died during infancy. Three married brothers were in business, and resided in the same house and the fifth was three years younger to Partap. Two sisters were married and the younger ones were at school. None of Partap's siblings had been to a college and everyone in the family expected him to go abroad for higher studies.

Two of the sisters, Tara and Urvashi, were our age group and most of my time was spent in their company. I liked the green-carpeted lawn in front and the open courtyard at the back. With horde of children, it was easy to make teams and play football or badminton or convert the dining table into a ping pong table. For the first time in my life, I appreciated the concept of a big family though sometimes I felt suffocated and missed the privacy I enjoyed at home. Once Tara, Urvashi and the two of us took bikes and had a ride through rain and thunder. We played cards, carom and ran around in the lawn.

Tara asked me to pick coriander leaves from the kitchen garden and I brought 2-3 times the quantity I used to buy from the market. She had a big laugh at my expense; their requirements were ten times the quantity I had plucked. I was dwarfed in that house by the immensity of numbers. For a boy confined to loneliness, I felt lost in the crowd.

Puzzled, I asked him, "How do you survive?"

"The accolades come in baskets if you achieve something and if you slip up, it is worse than brickbats."

One early morning, the two of us along with the girls, worked in the kitchen garden, prepared beds and planted the saplings bought from the nursery. I had never experienced this kind of camaraderie in my life and I envied Partap. We felt so buoyant, and full of synergy that we could have plucked at the stars.

Unable to get any sleep, one late night we spotted two rats chasing each other all over the room. Taking off our chappals, we aimed at the rodents, missed and ran after them creating pandemonium in the house. On hearing the footsteps, I turned and was stunned on seeing the master of the house.

"What is going on in the dead of the night?" He thundered. "Daddy — rats — two of them!" Partap muttered, trembling all over. "Shut up and go to sleep. Do you know what the time is? It is past two?"

Both of us scooted to our room, bolted it, laughed and laughed in the night mimicking his father. Whenever we turned and looked at each other in the night light, we broke into hoots of laughter. It continued till the next morning and stopped abruptly on overhearing his mother confide to one of her daughters, "Partap is getting very difficult in the company of his friend."

On return to Delhi, loneliness hit me hard. I encountered ma with why I didn't have any sibling? A little embarrassed, she turned the tables on me. "When you get married, have a dozen kids of your own."

"I will." I assured her. "At least the kids will have company."

It perturbed ma and she spent more time with me. But it did not help. I missed the comfort and the warmth of numbers in the family, someone to share one's thoughts, play and fool around: the feeling of togetherness, of family. The nostalgia of Meerut visit had a sweet scent and I often wrapped myself in it. Or whenever I remembered half a dozen family members at the dining table at Meerut, I wallowed in self-pity.

The only memorable holiday I had taken with papa was a year earlier at Andaman Islands. He treated me like an adult and taught me how to swim and snorkel. I loved the feel of splashing waves around me. With ma between us, we ran on the desolate beaches till she was exhausted. But I had not enjoyed the visit to Goa. I was about ten and my parents cuddled, necked, and had even kissed as soon my back was turned. His hairy hands on the bare legs of mother all the time had appeared revolting to me.

In tenth class, my visits to Jaipur decreased and I concentrated on my studies. My father turned up with his bag during the weekends and the two- bedroom flat felt overcrowded. His presence completed the family though I was aware it was temporary and he would leave on Sunday night. In my own little world I termed him `a weekend papa' or `a holiday papa'. After the Meerut visit, sometime I turned to my father desperately trying to hold on to whatever the little I had, and hugged him hard at the parting. However, I could not confide to him the problems of a growing up adolescent as we were not in that kind of comfort zone, which makes your inner thoughts tumble out. I was aware that he was concerned and threw loud hints at me; somehow, I remained tight-lipped and gradually with years, he gave up.

At ma's instance, I reciprocated the invitation to Partap.

"You are lucky to get undivided affection and attention of your mother. My parents sometimes forget in which class am I?" Partap complained and it confused me.

"But I like the atmosphere in your home -- so much love and warmth."

"There is lot of bitterness and pain also."

Partap was more matured and self- reliant than me. Ma liked my friend and he visited us often.

After the Meerut trip, I talked so much about Tara and Uravashi to my mother that she told me to make girlfriends in the school; we had over forty percent girls in our class. Aware of my shyness, she introduced me to some of the daughters of her colleagues. "Girls are more warm and affectionate than boys," she said. However, I was unable to bond with any girl. Partap continued to be my best buddy in school.

Ma was disappointed with my Senior Secondary result for she had been grooming me for the civil services. Partap made it to Engineering College, Roorkee, and I joined Hindu College in History (Honours).

Against the wishes of papa, ma bought a Maruti car. It was a momentous occasion. One early morning, we drove down to Jaipur and knocked at father's door unannounced. This was the only time he betrayed emotion of resentment on his face, and I felt happy to see him react like a normal human being. I was not sure whether he was upset because of the purchase of the car or the surprise element in our visit. When I mentioned of it to mother, she laughed it off saying, "You observe too much." Throughout the return journey she was pensive, nodding her head, or answering in monosyllables.

My enthusiasm for long drives took us more often to Jaipur and it delighted ma to see an expression of joy on my face. Every weekend, the two of us drove to some place nearby: Agra, Chandigarh, Haridwar, and Mussoorie.

Though I interacted with a large number of class fellows in the college, there was no one with whom I could relate or visit his home or take him into confidence. My inability to have a steady friend disturbed ma.

II

I was crestfallen when I could not make it to the IAS (Indian Administrative Service), ma, however, felt I was lucky to get Indian Audit and Accounts Service. It was during those days that she introduced me to Jaya, daughter of a colleague from the English department; Jaya had been selected in the IAS. Initially, I was lukewarm to Jaya but she made sure to run into me every day and her presence overwhelmed me. She dragged me to the movies, restaurants and we looked forward to seeing each other. Within a few weeks, I was besotted of her and we decided to tie the nuptial knot. Ma was hesitant only in one area: she was better placed than me. Jaya was short, fair and pretty and she had more brains. I dismissed mother's argument. "What more can I want?"

"Men are egocentric and women can lose their head if better placed. Keep this in mind before you finally get engaged."

Jaya and I were on cloud nine. She did not allow me to skid down to the earth and rationalize our relationship. We were engaged before we left for the National Academy of Administration at Mussoorie.

It did occur to me more than once that Jaya thought no end of herself and she overruled me with a sharpness bordering on arrogance. She noticed the frown on my face and clarified that being the eldest sibling she was given to admonishing and having the last word. The next time she repeated it and I winced, she cajoled me with a "Come on Hem, that's the way I am and you know I adore you," and I was made to shut up. During courtship, I did not want to rub it hard and allowed her to have her way.

We went through the marriage rituals promising to make it last till death. On our first posting at Chandigarh, we were at the top of the world. Dinners, parties, movies, the warm bubbly emotions, and a great sex- life: everything was in top gear. And I said goodbye to the loneliness with which I was obsessed since my childhood.

The trouble started in the fourth year with the birth of Manav. Our little world of happiness tumbled down. All our problems revolved around our darling baby. Taking care of him at night, keeping a watch on his growth and the crisis management required when he was not well. Jaya's complex office pressures of dealing with unreasonable politicians and an active media took their toll. She was bone weary by the time she reached home, and could not give any time to the baby. We had two full - time maids plus a nanny and I did my bit, but the child needed the care and warmth of a mother.

Fortunately, we shifted to Delhi. Our parents pitched in to look after the child and we moved on in life avoiding, dodging the unpleasant pinpricks and shards of life.

During the weekends, I played with my son on the carpet of the drawing room, and Jaya listened to the old songs. Sometimes she also joined and all three of us played with the ball as a complete family. I exulted in happiness and pride that I had a family of my own. I wanted to fill my son's life with basketful of joys and love and protect him from the rough winds of loneliness. I promised to myself that he would never feel lonely like me.

One day, her parents had taken away the little boy giving us a free evening to ourselves. I was on my second peg and wanted to discuss something and she wanted to play the new DVD movie she had brought while returning from the office. There are moments in our lives when we want to bare every nook and corner of our heart. I wanted to tell her about Partap, my trip to Meerut, and my feelings on return. I had tried it 3-4 times earlier and she had dismissed it with her usual gesture of hand as if pushing away a pest. The movement of her hand had annoyed me earlier but I had ignored it for the sake of peace at home. Now, she again gesticulated to stop the nonsense, pressed the 'play' of remote, settled down on the sofa and crossed her legs looking forward to the bliss of watching 'Izazzat', a movie she had missed viewing in the theatre.

"I want to talk to you, darling."

"Some other time," she answered.

I persisted, maybe unreasonably and she continued to ignore me. In sheer frustration, I switched off the DVD player and threw the remote on a sofa.

"Why???" She got up from the sofa, her arms on the waist and glared at me. "What's so great about the bloody Meerut trip you took more than 14-15 years back that you can't allow me to see a movie, which you damn well know I want to see?"

Flabbergasted, I muttered, "It's important to me, Jay."

"I know what happened there!" She mocked and ridiculed me, narrating almost everything I wanted to tell her. Jaya was excellent at theatrics, and she mimicked and dramatized every detail of the various incidents I had confided in ma.

"And I know what you are going to ask me?"

In anger, her black eyes turned small, her delicate face contorted and she looked ugly. "You want me to give you a dozen children like Partap's mother! Isn't it?"

I was about to leave when she caught my arm roughly and made me turn to face her fury. "Before you leave, you must know my reply so that you don't bother me again."

I stood like a blank wall.

"I have given you a son and you must be thankful to me for that. And no more children! If you wanted a dozen, you should have married a villager and not an IAS!"

"Thank you Jay for the clarification. Now you can see your movie."

I pressed the `play' of the remote, the TV screen turned alive and faces of Rekha and Nasirudeen Shah flickered on the screen and became steady. I struggled to my room and slowly closed it.

Her words hit me. It was like being served the same fledgling chicken in your childhood at dinnertime with which you had played in the morning. She had butchered the sweetest memories of my past. Memories, I cherished and was my support system.

Jaya did not see the movie. I heard her crying in the bedroom; I didn't make any attempt to mollify her.

It took us many weeks to break the ice and be our normal selves again. But the scars remained.

About six months later, I looked up one evening at the star-spangled sky and made another attempt to win her. It was the first of the moon and the evening star was adjacent to the moon. In striking contrast to the stars sparkling like diamonds, the moon was a dull yellow. Jaya too, was a little gloomy, a little sad. Swept by a wave of romanticism, I took liberties of using metaphors and said that she was the moon and I the evening star.

"I want you to be like the first of moon, and not like the full moon when the distance between the twain is the maximum. I know I am being selfish that I do not want you to reach the zenith of glory but that's the way I want it to be."

Jaya's expression was cold, perhaps wondering at my stupidity.

I was certain that I would be able to please her and continued to be poetic.

"Oh moon! Where doth thou wander,

Alone and palely loitering?

Art thou pale for weariness

Of climbing heaven —"

Jaya stared angrily at me and I stopped abruptly.

"You are mixing up Shelley and Keats." She snubbed me. Turning her head towards the sky, she recited P.B. Shelley's 'To the Moon' and John Keats' La Belle Dame Sans Merci verbatim.

Her each word was like a hammer. The contempt in her voice made me fall from the celestial heights. It was a slap on the face of an ignoramus.

A student of electrical engineering, Jaya had the audacity of an academia in literature.

After the above incident, I developed a hard exterior, lost my sensitivity and stopped bothering about anyone including my wife. And I made it a point to flaunt my indifference at the world. The only exception I made was in case of my son. I still cared for him. Jaya was not happy with my new approach to life, but she did not retaliate for she was aware that she had been instrumental in shaping it. I was worried that our relationship would snap any time.

My boss sent me for a six-week reorientation program at the Staff College, Shimla and I asked Jaya to accompany as we had fond memories of the hill station.

The trip was a disaster. The car broke down between Karnal and Ambala on the highway and no help was forth coming. It was my responsibility to get the car serviced but unfortunately, it had slipped out of my mind.

"I knew it!" She flared up. "You always let me down. Why can't you plan things properly, Hemanshu?"

I had no defence. I begged many truck drivers to tow our car to Ambala; they refused. Jaya, as usual, was more resourceful. She called the highway patrol on the mobile, introduced herself and asked them to arrange the car to be taken to Ambala. A jeep reached within 15-20 minutes. Our car was got repaired on priority while we rested in the circuit house. During the journey, she ridiculed me and threatened never to go on a holiday with me. By the time we reached Shimla, it was past ten in the night.

My maternal uncle, a retired professor of Political Science at Chandigarh University, had moved from Chandigarh to Shimla, and settled down in the old ancestral home and given it a semblance of respectability by carrying out renovations. He phoned in the morning and invited us for a cup of tea. Jaya had never been to the place; to please me, she agreed, though reluctantly.

Located between the Grand Hotel and the Head Post office on the road to Kali temple, the building had the smell of fresh paint. The ground floor was occupied by a small primary school. The wooden structure creaked as we ascended and went around the house. We were shown my ma's room and the attic where I along with other children had played once and finally took our seats in the large drawing room overlooking the Mall road. The backside window provided a splendid view of the mountains and the valley below. My uncle proudly mentioned that the house was more than a hundred years old and was got constructed by an Englishman. Jaya was brutal in her condemnation of the dilapidated house and uncle vainly tried to defend; his voice quivered with emotion.

My aunt brought the tea tray and after taking a sip of the hot cup, his tone turned conciliatory.

"To me, taking a warm cup of tea in this house invariably conjures up thoughts of the man who got the building constructed. What his attitudes would have been? His life style, habits and hobbies. A building speaks of the rulers, the locals, the inhabitants of this house and the entire culture and civilization of those times. Don't you think so?"

My aunt offered us fresh potato rolls.

"Even if you don't go so far in the past, at least your husband was born here — a small part of his childhood is buried in this old building."

"The old must give place to the new, uncle. Sentimentalism is a hindrance in progress. The house deserves to be pulled down and a posh hotel constructed."

"As it is, bureaucrats are bad enough — look at the mess they have created in this town and the country — but you speak the language of an estate agent!" Uncle was scathing and unreasonable.

Jaya could not stand the criticism, lost control of the situation and babbled incoherently. Finding her in a spot, I came to her rescue and finally rounded up the discussion. "Uncle, heritage apart, Jaya's suggestion deserves a second thought."

By walking on the fence, I displeased both of them. My uncle was so cut up that he did not come down to see us off.

Back in the staff college, Jaya fumed and fretted for not adequately defending her. "What sort of a husband do I have, who enjoys his wife being put on the mat?" Once triggered, she did not know when to stop, and continued on and on.

There was some element of truth in her accusations, for I gloated on her getting a taste of her own medicine. In the late evening, she sulked in the room refusing to budge out and I went for a long walk by myself.

Jaya cancelled her planned program to Chail on the flimsy plea that she had suddenly remembered something urgent at Delhi, and drove back. I didn't approve of her whims, but she ignored me. I realized that we were gradually drifting away from each other. Of late, our wrangles had increased; I too was unable to control my temper and gave it back to her, which escalated trivial incidents to crisis situations. The visit to my uncle had widened the chasm between us.

Of her own accord, she revisited during the third weekend, and we went to Chail. She was quiet and absent minded during the trip as if unable to resolve some enigmatic problem. When I mentioned it to her, she did not respond. Our stay at the Palace Hotel was dull. She looked lackadaisical in the photographs I took of her and Manav. The rich green lawn with varied blooming flowers, a walk through the thick forest clustered with deodars and other cypress trees or my singing the latest remix for my son: nothing lifted her spirits. I pointed out the bright red rhododendrons to her on the return journey to Shimla, but she continued to be insipid, lost in her own thoughts.

On the completion of the program, my boss, asked me to accompany her to a tour of a southern state. Major financial irregularities were noticed in the functioning of the State Govt. and a team was set up by CAG (Comptroller and Auditor General) and my boss was to lead it. I was not given time to visit my home and took flight from Chandigarh. The expected time frame of completing the exercise was a fortnight, but as we progressed, we unearthed major scams and took more than a month.

When I returned home, I noticed an unfamiliar Honda Accord parked outside my home. Jaya introduced me to her guest Madhusudan Sharma, an Associate Director at City Bank. He was an MBA from IIM, Bangalore. Taller than me, he had sharp features, big eyes, flawless complexion and was completely bald. He gave the impression of belonging to the upper crust of the society, the crème de la crème. Gracefully, he rose and shook hands with me. It made me a little uncomfortable that not only was he more youthful than me he was more at ease in my own home, which I had visited after almost three months. Jaya had changed the furniture, tapestry and the entire décor of drawing cum dining room and given it a finesse I didn't expect of her. Looking at the guest, I said, "It is good, isn't it?"

Madhusudan nodded, and turned his head away from me. I realized that somewhere I had made a faux pas, and worse, could not make it out. My confusion was so pronounced that Jaya said, "Madhu helped me in the selection of sofa, tapestry—."

"Oh?"

Madhusudan shifted uneasily at the incongruity of the situation and to diffuse the tension, was up on his feet. "Jay, I will make a move." Very politely, he shook hands with me and added, "Sir, I will come at some other opportune hour." He walked up to the door, turned his head towards my wife and moving his fingers as if playing a musical note, said casually, "I will give you a tinkle later."

Jaya nodded her head. She did not go up to the door to see him off, neither did I?

I wanted to say something nasty to take the load off my chest, but instead carried it to my bedroom. Discretion forced me in taking such a course, as I had learnt in life that when all the odds are against you, it's wiser to tread cautiously, one can slip even on firm ground. I looked at myself in the mirror, and realized I was death pale. Madhusudan's presence in my own home had threatened me. Intuitively, I knew something ominous was in store for me.

It was the first time in many years that we did not make love on meeting after such a long hiatus.

Jaya made sure to avoid me and often took dinner with Manav, and somehow I also felt more comfortable with the new arrangement though it did not last long.

One night, I told her that the Director, Staff College had hinted that he wanted me on the faculty.

"What have you told him?"

"I wanted to consult you."

"You decide what is good for your career," she said, switched off the light, and turned her head towards the wall.

She was turning edgy, almost desperate. I knew she had made up her mind on something and wanted to confide in me but could not take the plunge. "What is it Jaya?" I questioned her on 2-3 occasions. She slipped away making sure that I was unable to touch her.

Two days before Diwali, we sat in the drawing room during late evening; Manav was playing outside with his friends. Jaya had not switched on the lights, though twilight was approaching. We were watching a movie on aliens and she was jittery. Out of the blue, she rose, switched off the movie and sat down on the nearby sofa. Offended, I was about to retaliate when she mumbled, "I want divorce."

Stunned, I muttered, "What?"

I had feared it all the time.

She told me that she was in love with someone, wanted to marry him, and needed the divorce.

"Madhusudan," I said, almost in a whisper. She nodded, and added that she had known him for last two years.

"And Manav?"

"He will remain with me."

I sank deeper in the layers of the new sofa. How could she do it to me? At the back of my mind, I knew it was coming and had allowed the situation to drift.

"I am sorry." She moved closer and took my hand in hers. I jerked it away.

Darkness had crept in the room and invaded my life.

"I deserved better," I said grimly. "Manav also deserves more out of life. You have ruined his future."

I turned my head towards her and added bitterly, "I will give you divorce on the condition that I will keep the custody of Manav."

"I cannot live without him," she moaned, "and you know it." "You have to choose between Madhusudan and Manav."

My voice was hoarse, unlike my own.

Jaya argued that I didn't know how to handle a child, and maybe she was right. After my initial bravado, I gave in.

How would I live a life without Jaya and Manav? I feared that loneliness would again suck me. But I had no choice.

We filed the divorce papers in the court, and were granted divorce in about a year's time. I was given the right to see my child once in a week.

Ironically, the day we got the court orders, the same day I was promoted in Junior Administrative Grade; Jaya had been promoted six months earlier.

My parents stood by me during the crisis. The day the divorce proceedings were initiated, I had moved to my mother's bungalow; she had recently taken over as the principal of the college.

Ma was not the cribbing kind. She never reproached Jaya on the divorce, though her own mother had insinuated her of being selfish.

I considered myself to be a tough person. I was surprised when I had a heart attack slightly paralyzing my left shoulder and arm. I was in the hospital for a fortnight. Along with Manav and her new born, Jaya visited me and spent more than an hour. She wanted to touch me, wanting to share my sorrow. I pushed her hand away, and barely restrained myself from hitting her.

III

I spent hours analyzing our marital relationship and what had gone wrong? Perhaps, Jaya did not have the sensitivity to appreciate others' feelings and interests; she was too much obsessed with herself. I gradually realized that our marriage was doomed to failure, our bonds despite the birth of Manav, lacked in fragrance of love and wilted under a little strain of an intruder.

My fears regarding the future of my son were misplaced; he was stronger than me and took our separation in his stride. Perhaps, with years, he grew fond of the man who had replaced me. The very thought was like a stab in my heart. Sometime, I felt that he was reluctant to go out with me to the park or a restaurant. I did my best to cheer him: bought him toys, games, presents, books and video games. But I was not able to win his affection. My relationship with my own son was less tangible than what mine had been with my father. Manav looked up to Madhusudan, he did not need me. My weekly visits, perhaps, caused more confusion in his little brain, and I reduced them to once a month.

Delhi did not interest me and I sought a transfer to Bangalore. I moved like a vagabond from one posting to another as if searching for something in my life that I had lost. My officers, subordinates and the staff found it difficult to adjust with me. My apathy to men, office staff, and places increased with months. Some of my colleagues were considerate and often invited me for lunch or dinner and I liked interacting with their families. Watching happy families smile and laugh pleased me. "You must marry," the wives of my colleagues told me. "Forget your first marriage, it was a bad dream." My mother was also keen that I should settle down in life. I refused to indulge in any discussion on this issue. Once was enough, I told myself, I did not want to be hurt again.

After four years, I was posted back to Delhi at the Headquarters. Ma was due to retire by the end of the year and papa was younger to her by a couple of months.

It was the end of July. Monsoon had invaded Delhi and the sky was overcast with dark clouds; strong winds made them race away in the sky. I had yet to join my new assignment and was lazing in the balcony with the newspaper when ma looked at the sky with a mischievous smile, and asked, "Are these clouds not going to Jaipur?"

I looked at her quizzically and inquired whether she was not going to the college.

"I am bunking it," she answered with a frivolous air. "Let us give your papa a surprise."

In less than half an hour, we were on the Jaipur Highway. It was like old times: my mother chatting, offering me chips, 'kurkares', fruits and cold drinks and making cryptic comments as I raced the car to over a hundred.

"So much has gone by since those old times," she said touching my hair lightly. "Hem, you have aged."

"Hey! So have you, old lady!" I laughed trying to match her spirits.

Repeated pressing of the bell elicited no response from papa. I checked the veranda switches and concluded there was a power break down. No one opened the door though I banged it time and again.

Mother went to the back window and peeped in the bedroom. Her face turned white as if she had seen a ghost. "Let us go," she shouted from a distance and ran towards the car. I thought that the old woman had gone batty, and defying her, peeped inside. A young woman and my father were having sex. I realized that she must be one of his research scholars; ma often had a dig at him that he had only girls as PhD students. From the rear- view mirror, I saw papa rushing out, tying the shirt buttons and shouting, "Hem, Hem!" and waving frantically at me.

"Move," ma screamed.

I obeyed.

She wept throughout the return journey and refused to take anything. The halva she had brought for my father was disposed off in the garbage. We reached home after eleven in the night amidst a thunderous storm that was milder compared to what she had undergone.

When I opened the door for the milkman in the morning, I noticed my father hiding behind him. With a broad guilty countenance spread all over his face, he stood under a light drizzle: tall, fair and cherubic. Despite the unusual circumstances, he had managed to retain the intellectual air. It occurred to me that his research scholars must have considered him handsome. His dishevelled hair and wet clothes made him look almost youthful. In contrast, my mother was dark and thin to the extent of projecting a famished look and had no sex appeal. She had sharp features, attractive eyes with infinite depth, and a pretty smile: it was not sufficient to hold her man. It had been raining since last night, and I wondered for how long he had been standing outside the door unable to gather the courage to press the bell. It aroused my sympathy.

"Come, papa," I said softly.

He hesitated, he was afraid of the approaching avalanche. I caught his arm gently, brought him inside the home, and closed the door.

"Who is it?" Ma shouted from the kitchen.

Not getting any response, she angrily barged into the drawing room. Perhaps, she had expected him. "Why have you come?" She bellowed at him. "There is no place for you in this home."

Ma was given to shouting. She loved to show off her temper at home and in the college campus. After the initial outburst, she suddenly became quiet. I did not like the abrupt change in her. However, she did not allow papa to spend the night at her home, my attempts at reconciliation failed.

Papa stayed at a friend's place, and for a week kept on knocking at our door, apologizing with folded hands. Unable to assuage the hurt feelings of his wronged wife, he went back to Jaipur.

Ma lost her equipoise after the incident and grew a little weird. She did not attend the college after that day and proceeded on long leave.

Many a time she asked me to get married. "Without me, you will be very lonely in life, Hem" She was genuinely worried how I would survive in this world? I stopped arguing with her and said "Yes, ma," to everything she wanted. One day, she looked at me with her sad, liquid eyes and muttered, "Everything in life is temporary: love, togetherness, family —."

Ma had a massive heart attack, I feared it all along. Papa was away to Manila to attend a seminar, by the time he arrived, she was no more. Before her death, she had taken my hand in hers and said, "I don't blame him for anything. I had you — he had no one. It was but natural—. Tell him that I have forgiven him."

Papa was present at all the ceremonies and dutifully discharged the responsibilities of a husband. Jaya too brought Manav to attend the last rites of his grandma.

I saw off my father at the bus stand and told him about ma's last words. He did not offer any reply; maybe, he had reached a stage when it had ceased to have any meaning for him. He embraced me, and quietly sat down in the bus beside a youthful woman. Draped in a sari, she looked dignified and prettier than when I had seen her last time at Jaipur. As the bus turned, I waved and realized that I had bid goodbye to the man I had known as my papa.

IV

The pain in my left shoulder and arm that had been giving me problem since my heart attack grew much worse after mother's death.

"Hem, you must see an orthopedic surgeon soon." Jaya called one day. Her concern baffled me. Perhaps, she had seen me clutching at my arm at ma's funeral. I assured her I was fine, but she had already fixed an appointment with Prof. A. Gupta of All India Institute of Medical Sciences (AIIMS). I did not approve of her domineering methods as now she had no right on me. She sensed it, and apologized. "If it suits you, I would confirm with him." I was in pain and needed some medical advice, her contacts were invariably better than mine, and I yielded.

Prof. Gupta gave me lot of time and undivided attention. His bald head and wise eyes assured me that I was in one of the best hands in the country. He listened to me and nodded frequently. He scribbled something on the prescription slip. "You may have to blow lot of money for I am recommending you to a private physiotherapist. Be a little patient with her, she has the reputation of having a short temper but she is the best in her field. And very expensive."

I thanked him, and cross-checked: she had excellent credentials. I fixed an appointment with the receptionist at the Khurana Physio therapeutic Centre. The centre was in more than a thousand square meter bungalow at Defence Colony. The reception was not as spacious as I had expected though there were more than half a dozen patients. The receptionist talked to someone on the phone, walked over to me and said "Madam will see you in ten minutes."

In less than five minutes, I was ushered into the office of the doctor who ran the place. It was a small elegant office. A tall, fair lady with a long pleasant face, hair tied into a knot and wearing a white doctor's apron smiled professionally at me. I sat down on the only chair in the room.

"Yes, Mr. Nanda."

I smiled back at her, handed over the prescription slip on which Prof. Gupta had scribbled my problems. She glanced at the sheet, went through the MRI reports and again riveted her cold eyes at me. I told her about the heart attack, the umpteen hospitals and physiotherapy centres I had been to, and the pain I had when I moved my arm or the shoulder. Even driving was painful.

"I am told by Prof. Gupta that there is magic in your hands — I hope it works on me."

"Prof. Gupta is a dear friend of my father and is given to exaggeration. The way he talks, some of my patients suspect that he gets a cut from me." She smiled.

I raised my eyebrows.

"You are a very special person. Not only Prof Gupta but Jaya Sharma, an IAS officer in Finance Ministry, who was my patient sometimes back, also called up. Are you related to her?"

"Sort of."

Jaya had not left anything to chance, she was efficient as usual.

The doctor rose from the seat and I noticed that she was in grey faded jeans. "Come."

She opened a door and we entered a huge hall containing about 10-12 beds; most of them were occupied by patients. Half a dozen girls and boys in white apron were attending to them. She walked to a spare bed in a corner, and told me to remove my shirt. She threw her coat on a chair and I noticed she was sporting a sleeveless black top with thin straps. I lay down on the bed and her hand moved on my shoulder raising my arm, trying to ascertain the extent of pain I could bear. She spent some time twisting my arms in various positions. I was conscious of her exuding sensuality as she leaned on me, touching, exploring the different areas of my shoulder and arm.

"It's going to take a couple of months and it is expensive." She told me a certain amount, which was not too much of a hole in my pocket. Her voice was crisp. "Twice a week –Tuesday and Friday. Be here in the evening before six, we close down at seven. Does it suit you?"

"Yes, doctor." I thanked her and left.

I was first exposed to Interferential Therapy (IFT) in which a low frequency current was passed for about ten to twelve minutes, followed by water fomentation. Dr. Priti Khurana or some other young physiotherapist did the mobilization exercises. Then I was told to rotate the wheel fixed to the wall, pull the string across a pulley system and move my hands up a staircase fixed to the wall. Later, I was given a weight of one kilogram and told to perform 6-7 exercises. It almost took me an hour to complete the entire schedule drawn by Dr. Priti. Even if she did not perform the mobilization exercises, she made it a point to inquire the progress. When I continued to say, "No," after a month, she was worried and took charge of my treatment.

A part of the mobilization exercises involved her applying pressure (like kneading the flour) on the joint of the arm and the shoulder with my arm suspended in the air making me feel uneasy. In such a position, the left arm of the physiotherapist was close to my hand. One day, I took courage and asked her, "Mind if I catch hold of your arm."

"Not at all." Her tone was flat.

Holding of her bare arm became a part of the schedule.

With advent of winter, the number of patients dropped in the late evening and I was the only one in the hall. It must have been financially unviable to use air conditioners in such a big hall and I was asked to use the bed in the room of Dr. Priti. She was invariably in the same jeans, the tops changed from black to white and rarely to red. Except for talking about the improvement in the condition of my arm, she never asked me anything. Her face was emotionless, her hands, bare arms moved like a machine.

Once, I noticed she was melancholy and was unable to hide her feelings. During the mobilization exercises, she used to pull at my hand in the opposite direction trying to make my grip strong. When she did it that day, I smiled and said, "I don't know whether I'll improve or not but you are surely going to have stronger muscles."

There was something in the way I said it that she had a belly laugh and her eyes grew wet. Priti went back to her chair, wiped the tears and shaking her head murmured, "What a thing to say?"

Laughing, I rose from the bed and sat down opposite her. After she was composed, I ventured to inquire why she was sad.

Without answering me, she picked up the phone and asked the receptionist to send in two coffees. It was the first time I was being treated to coffee. "Let us complete the routine," she said.

We started from the same exercise, she exerted pressure on my hand and again she was unable to control her hysteria. "I must be getting crazy," she said and went back to her chair. I also could not suppress my laughter. She picked up a magazine from the side table and tried to concentrate on it. I took the weights and went through all the exercises with my back towards her.

Coffee arrived, and she offered it to me.

"Sometimes, one behaves like a child," she said. "You have transported me to my childhood days."

Her eyes again swelled with tears. "Thanks, Mr.Nanda. I have not laughed like this in last ten years."

I wanted to share with her similar experience of the night at Meerut when Partap and I had laughed our heads off, but hesitated as I hardly knew her.

Next day, after we were through with the exercises, she looked at her watch and told me that her husband wanted to talk to me. A few minutes later, a youngish looking man, lightly built, with a prominent moustache opened the door with a warm "Hello!" Attired in jeans, blue shirt and a casual cardigan, he had a twinkle in his eyes. "I am Shashi, your doc's husband." He smiled affably and looked handsome. "Let us go inside, this room is unsuitable for a friendly chat."

Priti needed some time to wind up and told us to go ahead.

At the end of the hall, he opened the door to a spacious drawing room. Big oriental sofas in soft floral pattern dominated the room tiled in off white colour. The singular arrangement of lights and exclusive embellishments impressed me and I paid a compliment to the master of the house. "You should tell it to Priti, she would be happy to hear."

He offered me a seat, sat down next to me, and pressed a switch hidden under the side table. "You won't mind tea."

A maid appeared and he gave some order. He was an engineer and wanted to go to Middle East and needed some help in the

Foreign Cell that dealt with Government — Government deputations.

I adopted the usual bureaucratic line of dealing with an unknown situation. "I will see what I can do — you can give me your particulars."

I looked at the watch giving a loud signal that I had lost my interest in him. If I were in my own office I would have perhaps dismissed him, unfortunately I was in his plush drawing room and didn't want to snap ties with his wife especially after we had struck a rapport yesterday. Shashi was familiar with the reflexes of government officials; he didn't give up.

"I am told that you know Deshpande, he is your batch-mate and a good friend of yours."

Realizing I was dealing with a pushy young man, I scowled. "You seem to know a lot about me."

"I know about you through Jaya. She is a friend of my wife."
"And Jaya told you about Deshpande."

He nodded.

It hurt me. The trap in which I had stepped in was laid meticulously. Of course, I was certain that Jaya could never stoop to such pettiness. I was in a dilemma whether to walk out or give a piece of my mind to my host.

I did neither.

Attired in a flowing red gown, her hair loose, a light touch of make-up, and sparkling jewellery, Priti walked in looking a stunner. I was mesmerized by the effect of the soothing lights on her. I rose as if I were meeting an unknown beautiful woman and wanted to be introduced to her. Shashi also rose and left the two-seat sofa and his wife sat down next to me.

"Will you tell Radha to prepare some cutlets?" She turned towards her husband.

After he had left, she said again, "I am sorry, but I am not a party to the manipulations of my husband. Oblige my husband only if you are not compromising with your dignity."

Now I was on surer grounds, the subject of deputation was not mentioned again that evening.

Priti's clarification mollified me and I liked her candidness. I thought about it and felt I was overreacting as I didn't lose anything by putting in a word to Deshpande. I spoke to him and he promised to check. After a fortnight, he informed that Shashi Khurana had a good CV and was likely to be picked soon.

A couple of weeks later, Shashi barged into the room. "Hey! I have been selected for Algiers. This calls for a celebration!"

He invited me for dinner and gave me all the credit though I admitted I had done nothing.

I was quite surprised to see her three children at the dining table; the eldest boy was eleven years, about Manav's age.

After that day, Shashi made sure that I did not leave the centre without dinner. I felt I was imposing on him and protested. Priti pressed her hand on my shoulder and I could not refuse her. I too started reciprocating dinners in the club and sometimes at my place. Gradually, I became fond of Shashi and the children, Priti continued to be the perfect hostess. Sometimes, she persuaded me to have dinner even in the absence of her husband.

My relationship with Priti changed. She dropped the professional mask of the cold woman with a sharp tongue. She wore it, to distance herself from the male clients. The relationship I developed with her had a placid ease, which I had not shared with anyone, not even with Jaya. Lying down on the bed, with my hand on her arm and her hands engaged in mobilization exercises on my shoulder, I unwound myself. I talked of the mundane activities of the office, my childhood, my parents and my relationship with them, my frequent visits to Jaipur and my loneliness. She kept no secrets from me, but never talked of her spouse and I never mentioned Jaya.

Her father had given her the plot of land after his death; the three brothers contested it in the court of law and as a compromise she had to pay money to her brothers. She had made heavy investments in setting up the centre, raised exorbitant loans and everything was mortgaged: the machines, equipment, furniture and even the sofas in her lounge. Her husband had been without a job for last two years and was a free lance consultant working from home. "I am hoping that Shashi would earn sufficient money to pay off the loans," she told me. She was rather vague about her plans of joining him as she did not want to give up her practice.

"Geographical distances between the couples can break up marriages," I said.

"I know."

She turned sad, and I caressed her hand.

I told her about the Meerut incident. "Why didn't you tell me the day I had gone crazy?" Her hand lingered on my shoulder a little longer.

The day she learnt that I was Jaya's ex- husband, she was a little surprised, and muttered, "I didn't know."

One evening I turned up late and Priti left me to do my routine and I took some time. I was also lost in my introspection as to why was I spending so much time with this family and where would all this end? By the time I reached the dining room, they were all seated and waiting for me expectantly. There sat Shashi Khurana at the head of the table surrounded by the warmth of the family, the children chattering, the wife smiling at him. Moved by the scene,

I sat down beside the eldest boy. Suddenly, it occurred to me that this picture was likely to be short lived as Shashi was leaving within a fortnight.

After my return to Delhi, I felt that I had distanced from my son still more and could not relate to him. I had an uncanny feeling that he resented my presence as if he was wasting his precious time with me. Twice, he had looked at the clock after an hour hinting that my time was up. I felt more comfortable with Priti's son than my own and it disturbed me.

On a bleak December morning, Shashi Khurana left for Algiers. I had also gone to see him off at the airport.

One day, as usual, Priti tried the hand pulling exercise, and was taken unawares when I was able to press her hand against the bed.

"That's it. We have done it, Hem!"

"Thank you."

"You would be your old self in a few visits," she said, and turned melancholy. "I'll miss you."

I knew I would miss her more. "Me, too"

I caught her hand, and gently kissed it.

My shoulder and arm movements were normal within two weeks and she invited me for a special dinner. "Come tomorrow, I will cook the food with my own hands."

By the time I reached her place, the family was already seated and Shashi's chair was empty. Casually, I walked over to my usual seat and was about to sit when the eldest boy said, "Why don't you take papa's seat?"

I sat down next to him and playing with his hair told him I was more comfortable by his side. The little girl seated adjacent to Priti also took up her brother's cause.

Priti intervened. "Come on Hem, you can sit here."

Awkwardly, I left my seat, went up to the chair and slowly lowered myself in it. The little ones clapped; I looked at them and smiled.

I wanted to say so many things: I was happy to be a part of this family, I had never felt more complete etc. But I didn't say a word, and kept my head down fearing that tears should not fall in the plate. The little girl kept on chirping, "Uncle, isn't mother's cooking excellent — no one and no one can beat her." The boy echoed, "Oh, she is the best mom in the world!"

I kept on nodding my head. I was so overcome by emotion that I had to rush to the toilet to wipe my tears. After the dessert, I said to my hostess, "Thank you Priti for an excellent meal. You really are the best." I shook hands with her. Her hand moved to my shoulder and patted me. "Whenever you feel like, drop in," she added before my car glided out of the portico.

There was not a single day I had not thought of her and the children and I missed them most on Tuesdays and Fridays. Twice, I had gone to her place, but did not stop the car and drove away straight. Once, a ludicrous idea struck me that I should pretend my right arm was also giving me trouble and visit her centre for treatment. But she was sure to catch me, I thought, and decided against it. Despite so much of friendliness and the physical proximity in our relationship, I had never kissed her. I wondered why I was such a coward.

Six months later, I got a phone from her inviting me to join for dinner. "We are all missing you," she added.

We had a meeting with the Public Accounts Committee, the Parliamentarians continued to discuss the irregularities pointed in the CAG Annual Report, and I was delayed. By the time I reached, the children had already taken their meals. After the kids were nestled in the bed, Priti and I had a quiet dinner. Dressed in a peach coloured sari and a matching sleeveless blouse, she looked bewitching though sombre.

"Let us take the coffee in the garden." She suggested.

It had been a gruelling day in the office and I was exhausted. The August sky was overcast with dark grey clouds and my spirits soared when the wind breezed past the `neem' tree creating musical susurration. I expected she would break her silence and talk about herself. Maybe, the time span of six months had snapped the spontaneity in our relationship. I decided to help her out, and lightly touched her bare arm.

"Hem, sometimes, it gets very lonely in the house without a man. I miss Shashi all the more because he worked from home."

The sky blazed with lightning in the south west.

"Yes, you must be missing him." I took a sip of the warm coffee. Priti again turned quiet and kept on stirring the sugar with a spoon. It irritated my sensibility though I liked the frequent wafts of breeze, the lightning and the roar of clouds in the backdrop.

"The bastard!" She hissed in the night.

I could hear it over the thunder of the clouds.

And then she cried. Her loud sobs echoed in the night. I rose from my chair, threw my arms around her, and she kept on crying. My hand continued to wipe her tears, caress the arms. Composed, she spilled the beans.

During the period Shashi was unemployed in India, he had become friendly with an old colleague, a divorcee, who wanted to marry him. He had flatly refused for he did not have any such emotions for her. "Now I am told by someone — I could be wrong — that Revati (the divorcee) has flown to Algiers for a month on some UNDP project."

Priti finished her cup, and I poured some hot water and milk in it. I suspected that the ground reality was much worse than what she had confided in me.

"I know she is getting desperate. I don't know whether my marriage bonds are strong enough to withstand her affection, especially when I am not there."

"Everything would be fine," I said. "After all, the children are with you."

"No, it is not helpful beyond a point. If Jaya could do it, so can Shashi."

It made me shut up though it was not intended to be a snub. A gust of wind swept everything away: the tablecloth, the kettle, the cups and saucers. The maid rushed and carried away the crockery. We continued to sit in the wicker chairs with the wind lashing around us.

"If it comes to the worst, you can lead your own life — perhaps with me," I said thoughtfully, choosing every word carefully.

"I have never thought of a life without Shashi. I love him."

Her words rang out in the night, reverberating in the cosmos. My face turned stark white. There was a continuous flash of lightning above our heads, almost blinding us. She rose and touched me on the cheek, and whispered, "Hem! I did not know you loved me—."

The cloudburst in the heavens was like an explosion; bewildered, she fell in my arms and I held on to her. A drizzle sent me to raptures. I could not control myself and kissed her hard.

With it came rain. Hard rain.

"Tonight, the elements have gone berserk. I don't think it is advisable to go home in this weather," she said.

Sadly, I looked at her and walked towards my car. She caught my arm, and kissed me lightly. "If ever in life, I am free and single, I will call you."

My face lighted up, and I nodded.

That was about five months back. I am still waiting for her phone, still hoping to get a family.

■■■

Acknowledgements

My daughter Shikha presented me Jhumpa Lahiri's Interpreter of Maladies on one of my birthdays; it motivated me to write the short fiction. Many thanks for your gift, my dearest.

Some of us from our batch meet once a month over lunch — we have been doing it for over a decade — and the host has to speak on any subject of his choice; I have been reading my short stories. I am grateful to the members of our group for listening to my stories patiently and giving their valuable feedback, which has helped me to improve on the stories. Many thanks, friends.

I am thankful to Mike Flannery, Editor, 8th day, The Statesman and Niharika, Editor, Sunday Magazine, The Pioneer for giving me a break in their newspapers and publishing my short stories.

Sushma has spent many long hours in editing the stories and the book. 'In Turmoil' has got its present shape only because of her efforts. Many thanks, my life partner!

Thanks to Dr A Gupta, the publisher and his team; and special thanks to my friend Dr Atul Jain.